MOVIE MADNESS!

A GOLDEN BOOK • NEW YORK

Meet Buzz Lightyear and Sheriff Woody!

Rex is a T. rex and Hamm is a piggy bank.

Say hello to Slinky Dog and Bo Peep.

Woody loves to play with Andy.

Woody has a special spot on Andy's bed.

The other toys listen to Woody.

Rex is a lovable dinosaur!

Hamm protects Andy's coins.

Happy birthday, Andy!

Woody is eager to meet Andy's new toy.

Buzz Lightyear is a space ranger.

To infinity . . . and beyond!

Andy wants to be a space ranger, too.

Buzz and Rex get along well together.

Uh-oh! Buzz takes a fall.

Hold on tight, Buzz!

Woody is *not* happy with Buzz.

Buzz and Woody put on clever costumes.

Toy Aliens are prizes in the Rocket Ship Crane Game.

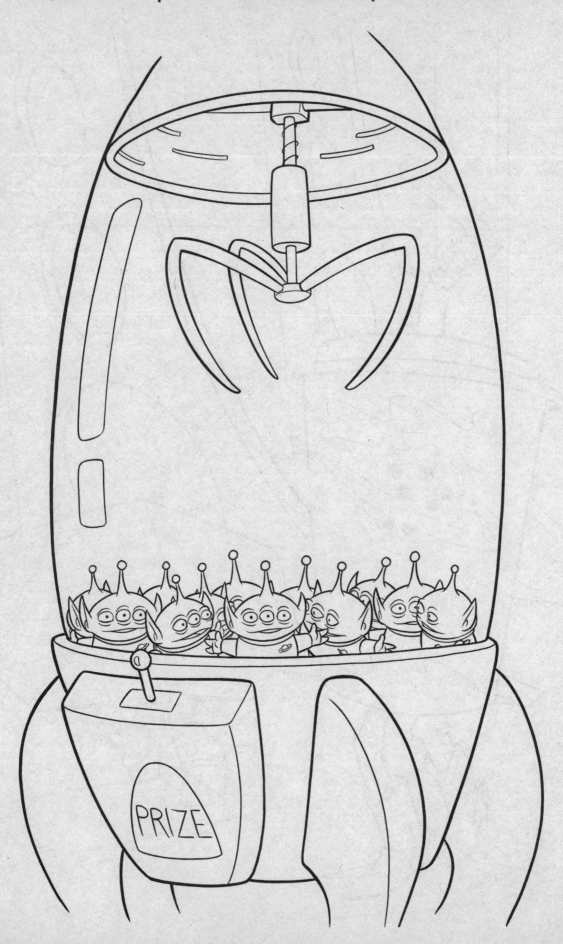

The Claw has chosen Buzz and Woody!

Sid is Andy's mean neighbor!

Buzz and Woody are trapped in Sid's backpack.

Buzz and Woody back away from Sid's mutant toys.

Sid has one scary collection of toys!

Sid is eager to use his new rocket—on Buzz!

Buzz and Woody had better escape soon!

Sid gets ready for blastoff.

Woody gives Sid a big surprise.

Sid is terrified!

The toys' plan worked!

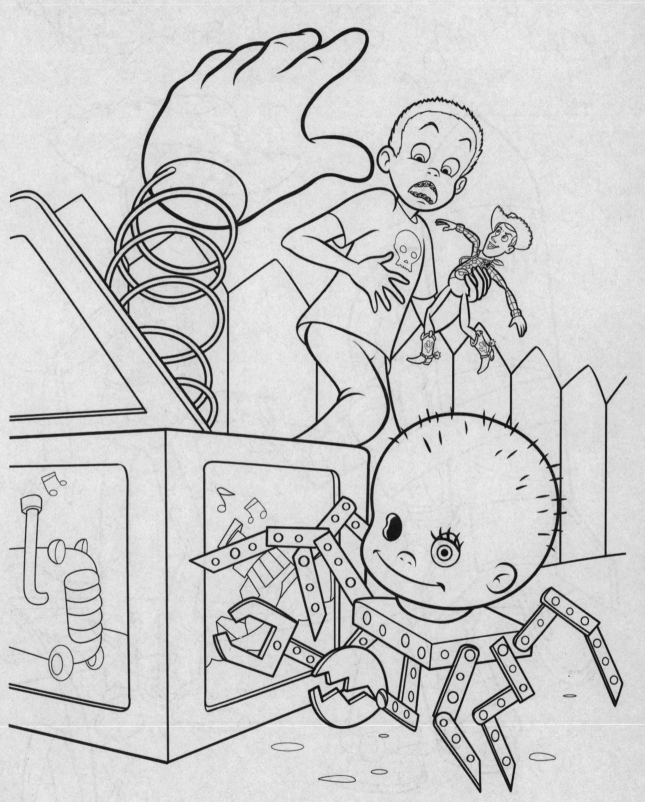

Buzz is thankful for Woody's help.

Andy misses Buzz and Woody.

Oh, no—Andy is leaving!

Buzz and Woody have to catch the moving truck.

The toys have to hurry!

Buzz tries to give Woody a helping hand.

Andy's toys are on the lookout for Buzz and Woody.

RC drives to the rescue.

Buzz and Woody soar through the air!

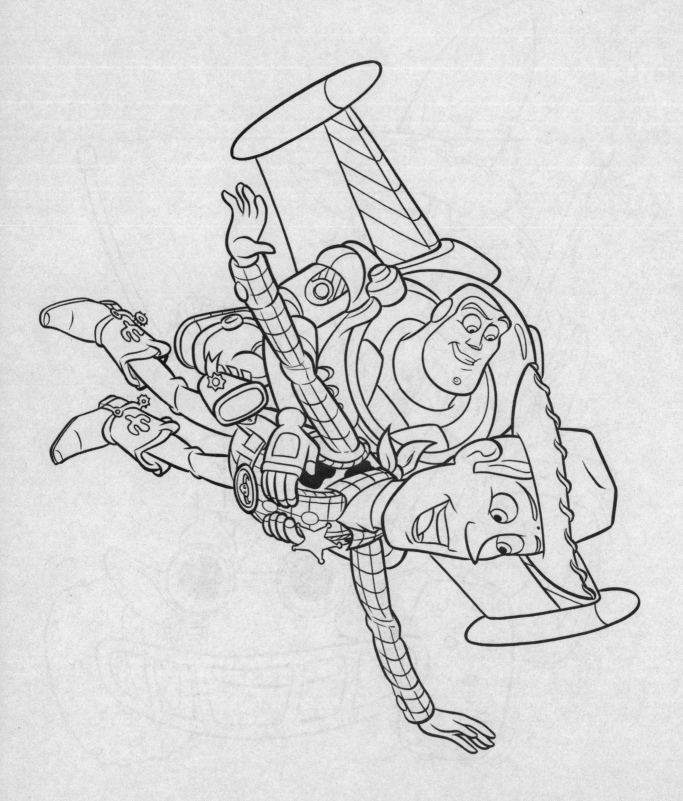

Andy is happy to see Buzz and Woody!

Buzz and Woody are glad to be back with Andy.

Andy's toys gather around his TV.

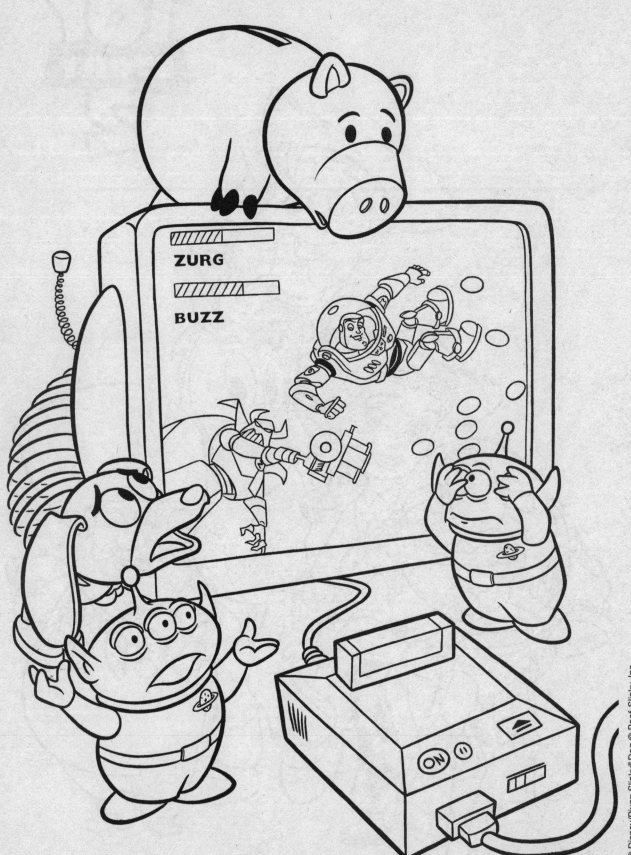

ZURG

BUZZ

Rex loves to play video games!

Andy has fun playing with his toys.

Riiip—Woody's arm has torn!

Woody can't believe Andy is leaving for Cowboy Camp without him!

Wheezy is a penguin toy with a broken squeaker.

Andy's mom is having a yard sale—
and Woody gets stuck in the middle of it!

Al the toy collector steals Woody!

Buzz won't let Al get away without a chase.

Woody meets the Roundup gang!

The Prospector greets Woody.

Woody once had his own TV show.

Jessie is very sad.

Jessie's owner gave her away many years ago.

Al's Toy Barn is a big toy store.

Buzz leads the way.

Hamm and Rex explore Al's Toy Barn.

Rex prepares to defeat Emperor Zurg!

The toys cruise the aisles.

It's a brand-new Buzz Lightyear!

Buzz meets . . . himself!

New Buzz is not very friendly.

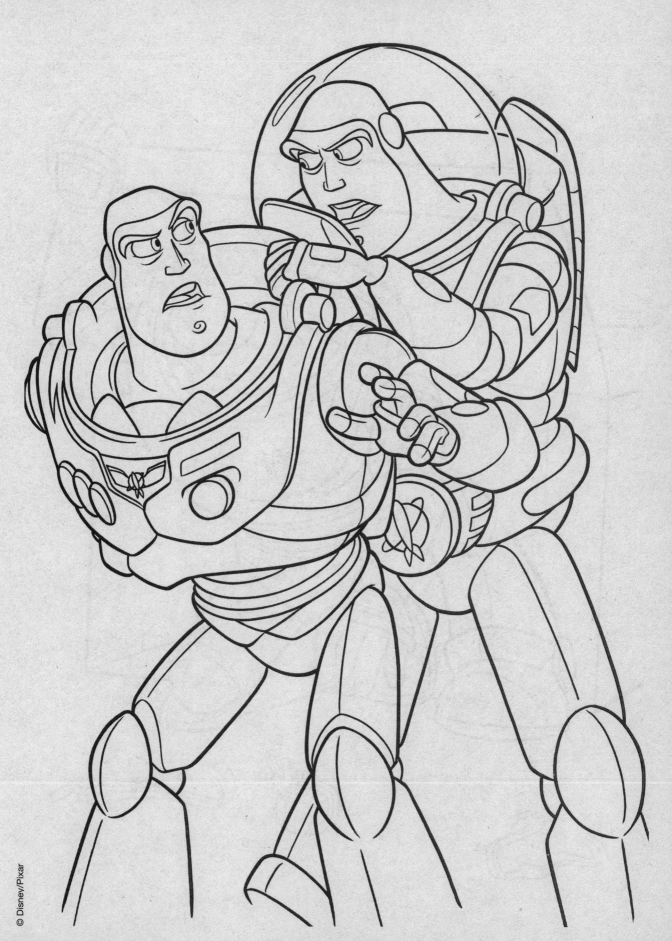

Buzz breaks out of his box.

The toys have to hurry!

The Roundup gang is in for a surprise.

Buzz reveals his true identity!

Woody is reminded of Andy.

Slinky stretches to help his friend.

The toys give each other a boost.

Which way should Buzz go?

Jessie needs help!

Woody is determined to save Jessie.

Woody has found Jessie!

Woody and Jessie need to get off the plane!

Buzz and Bullseye arrive just in time.

The toys celebrate a successful rescue!

Andy's toys welcome him home.

Buzz Lightyear to the rescue.

Draw a line from each picture to its close-up.

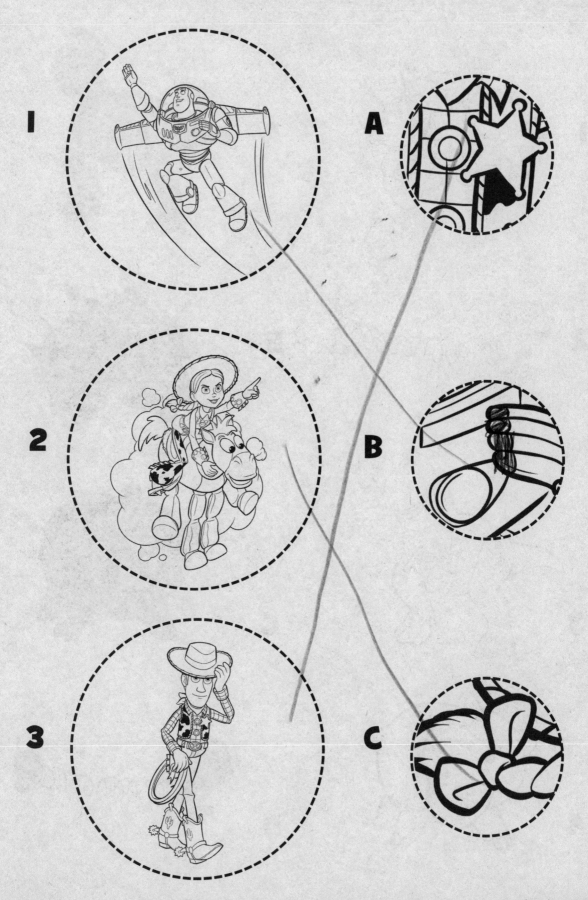

ANSWER: 1-B; 2-C; 3-A.

Draw a line from each toy to its shadow.

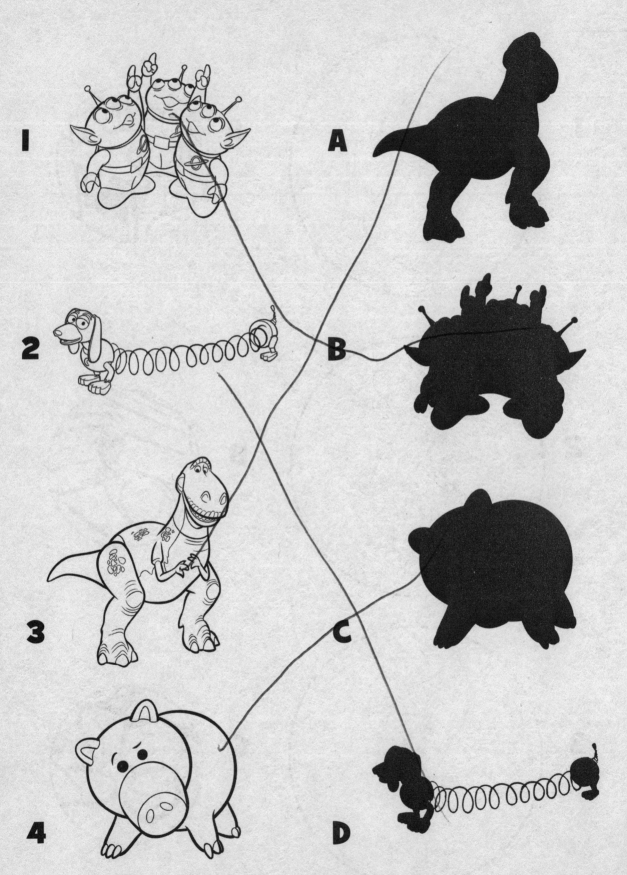

ANSWER: 1-B; 2-D; 3-A; 4-C.

When Andy was younger, he loved his toys—and playtime was always fun!

Now Andy is a teenager and doesn't play with his toys anymore.

Woody tells Rex that Andy still cares about his toys.

Color all the pictures of Buzz. How many are there?

ANSWER: 5.

Andy's mom thinks the big bag of toys is garbage.

Woody must find his friends before they are taken
away by the garbage truck!

How many garbage bags can you count?
Circle each one.

ANSWER: 10.

Jessie and her friends are going to a new home at the
Sunnyside Daycare Center.

Andy's mom takes the toys to the Sunnyside Daycare Center.

An old bear named Lotso is the leader of the toys at daycare.
Circle the cane that matches the one Lotso is holding.

It's time to meet a few of the daycare toys.
Here are Twitch, Chunk, and Sparks.

Woody uses a kite to fly away from Sunnyside.

A little girl named Bonnie finds Woody.
She takes him home to play.

Woody likes playtime with Bonnie and her toys.

Help Buzz find the right path to the door.
Watch out for the toddlers!

START

EXIT

ANSWER:

Cross out all the pictures of Buzz and Woody.
How many pictures of Lotso are left?

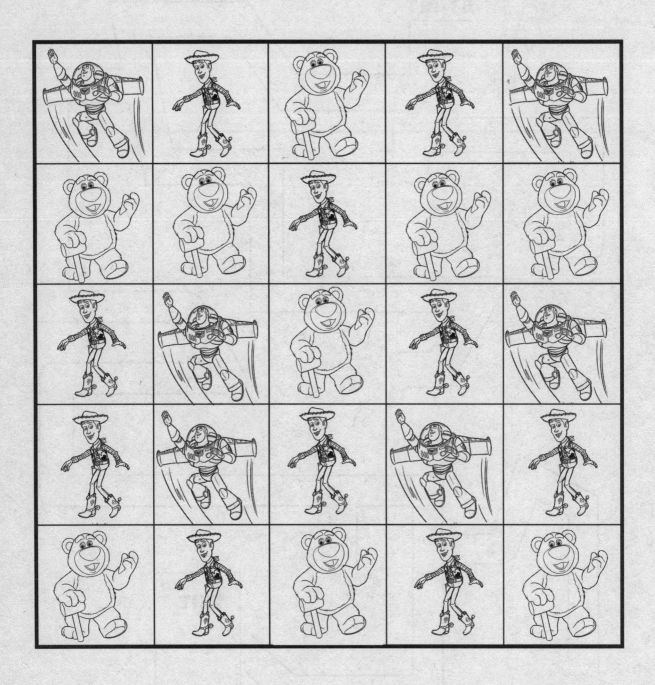

Chuckles tells Woody that Sunnyside is a bad place.

Using a yellow crayon, color all the stars that have the letters in Woody's name.

Woody is going to save his friends and take them back to Andy's house.

It's time for Andy's toys to leave Sunnyside. Which path leads to the garbage truck? Watch out for Big Baby!

All of the toys fall into the garbage truck.
They are taken away to the dump.

Find and circle these four objects in the picture below.

Andy's toys are pushed into a pile of garbage.

The toys are saved just in time!

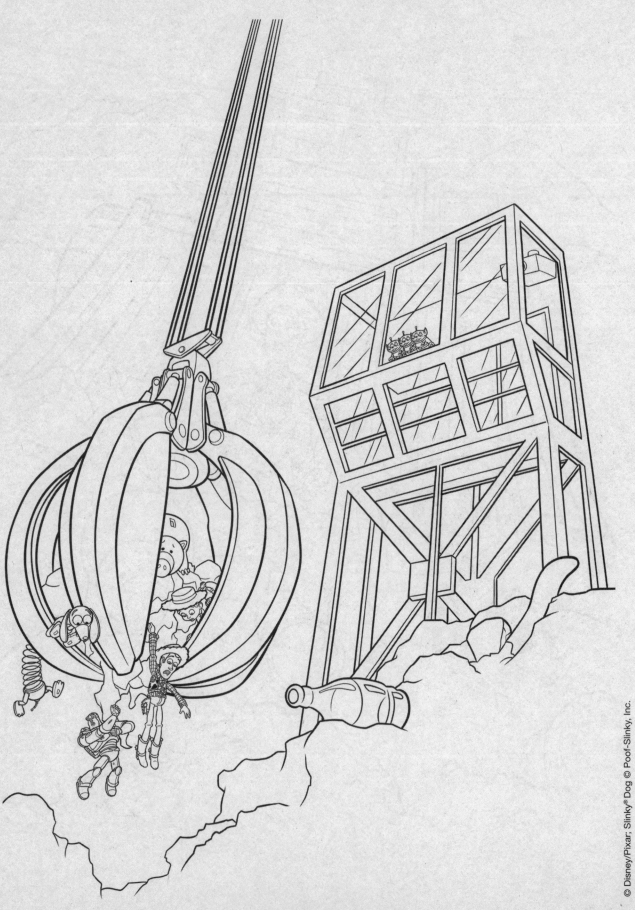

The Aliens are heroes!

Woody and Buzz say goodbye to Andy—and hello to their new life with Bonnie!

Sulley is the Number One Kid Scarer at Monsters, Inc.

Mike is his assistant. Scarers collect screams, which are turned into power for the city of Monstropolis.

Celia is Mike's girlfriend. She has snakes on her head instead of hair. Circle the picture that is different.

A

B

C

D

E

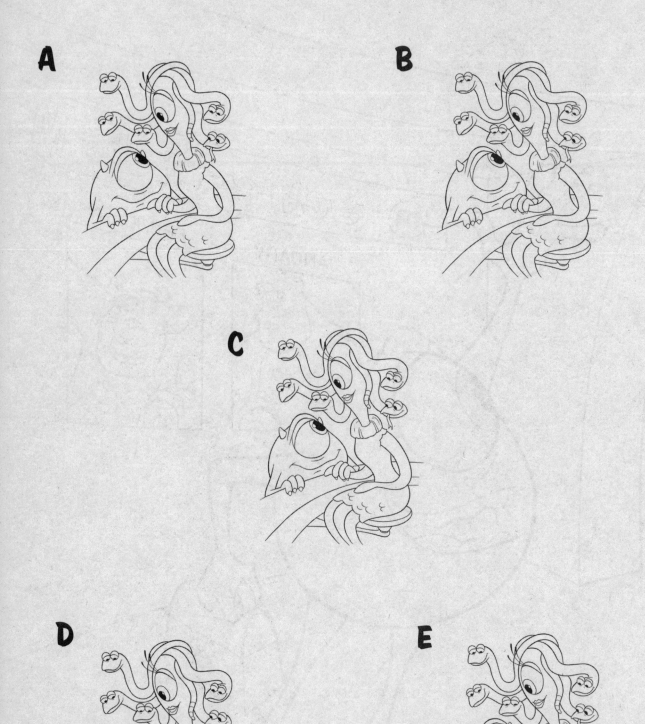

Randall is a Scarer, too. He can disappear
by blending into things. How many *R*s can you find
hidden in the picture?

© Disney/Pixar

Roz is in charge of paperwork. Mike never does his, and that makes Roz mad.

Mike can't do his work because he can't find a pencil. How many pencils can you find?

ANSWER: 5.

The top Scarers walk onto the Scare Floor.

The closet doors on the Scare Floor lead into kids' rooms.

Monsters are scared of kids. They think kids' belongings will hurt them! To find out what's scaring these monsters, unscramble the letters and write them on the blanks.

A   C   K   S   O

___ ___ ___ ___

ANSWER: A sock.

Sulley and Mike put kids' screams in special cans. How many words can you make by using the letters found in SCREAM? (Use each letter only once in each word.)

_____   _____

_____   _____

_____   _____

_____

_____

_____

POSSIBLE ANSWERS: Am, are, came, care, cream, ear, me, race, ram, and sea.

The Child Detection Agency (CDA) keeps
monsters safe from kids' stuff. They arrive
to take away the dangerous sock!

Waternoose is the head of Monsters, Inc. He asks Sulley to show the new Scarers how to be scary.

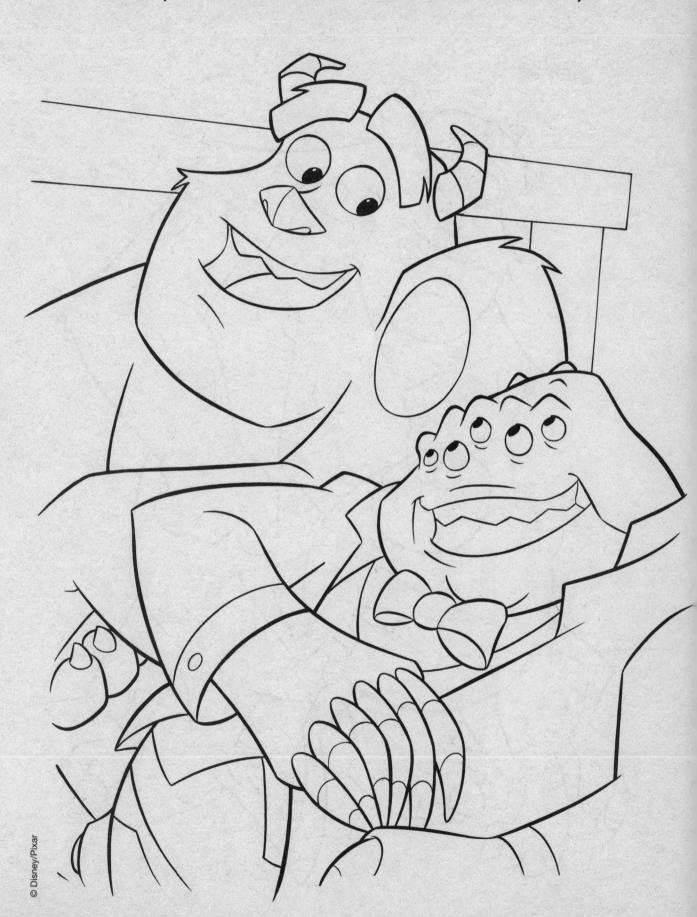

Roz is upset because Mike didn't finish his
paperwork. Sulley tells Mike he'll finish it for him.

When Sulley goes back up to Mike's desk, he sees
a door. Then he hears something behind him.
To find out what it is, circle every third letter. Then
write the letters in order on the blanks.

C X A N Q K B R I Z M D

___ ___ ___ ___

ANSWER: A kid.

Oh, no! A kid is in the monster world!

Monstropolis is in danger! Sulley has to
put the kid back in her own world.

Sulley doesn't want anyone to see him with a kid. He hides from Randall. How many Ss can you find in the picture?

Connect the dots to see
where Sulley hides the girl.

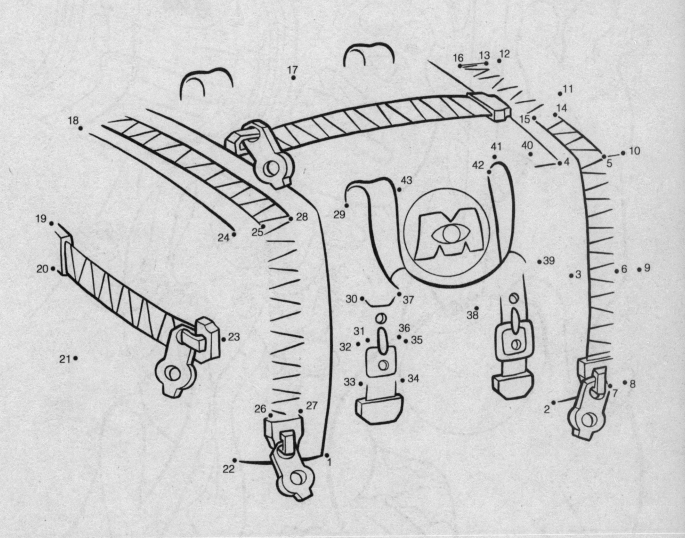

Mike and Celia are out to dinner
when Sulley appears at the window.

Sulley tries to show Mike the kid . . .

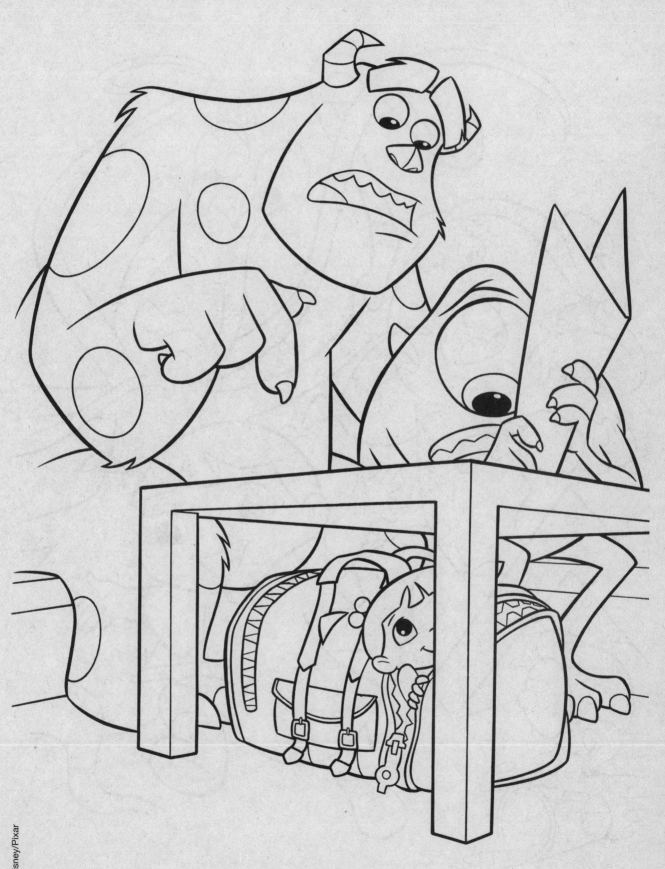

. . . but she has already gotten away!
All the monsters scream and run outside.

Mike and Sulley find the kid. To figure out where they take her, use the key to fill in the blanks.

1	2	3	4	5	6	7	8	9	10	11	12	13	14	15	16	17	18	19	20	21	22	23	24	25	26
A	B	C	D	E	F	G	H	I	J	K	L	M	N	O	P	Q	R	S	T	U	V	W	X	Y	Z

___ ___ ___ ___ ___ ___ ___
20   15   20   8   5   9   18

___ ___ ___ ___
8   15   13   5

© Disney/Pixar

ANSWER: To their home.

Mike and Sulley are scared of the kid.

When the girl screams, the lights go on and off.
When she laughs, the lights glow even brighter.
Mike's apartment is mixed up, and that makes the kid
giggle. Can you find everything that is wrong?

© Disney/Pixar

ANSWER: Mike's lamp is an umbrella; there is a plate on the chair; the clock on the walls has legs and feet; and the vase on the table has lollipops in it.

The kid draws a picture of a monster she's afraid of.
It's Randall! Use the key to color him.

Key

1 = RED	4 = GREEN
2 = ORANGE	5 = BLUE
3 = YELLOW	6 = PURPLE

The girl gives Sulley a special name.
To find out what it is, unscramble the letters
and write them on the blanks below.

T   Y   K   I   T

_ _ _ _ _

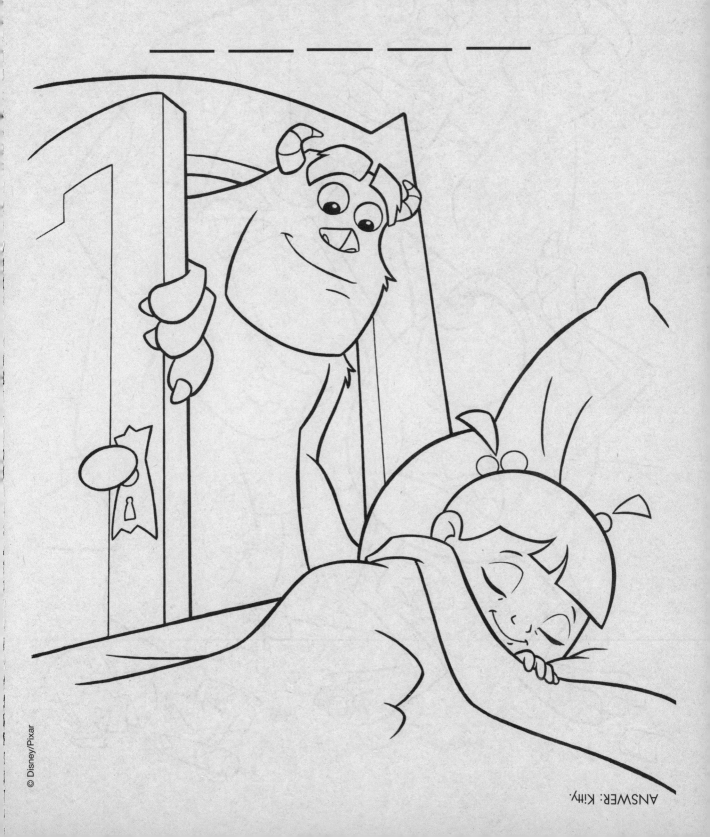

© Disney/Pixar

ANSWER: Kitty.

Sulley doesn't think the girl will hurt them.
Mike doesn't agree with him.

Sulley and Mike want to sneak the girl back into Monsters, Inc. What would be the best costume for her?

ANSWER: D.

The next day, Sulley and Mike take the girl to Monsters, Inc., so they can put her back in her room.

Sulley and the girl play hide-and-seek. "Boo!" she says.
Look at this picture carefully, then turn the page.

What is missing?

Randall wants to find the girl.
Mike and Sulley keep her hidden.

Sulley and Mike are looking for the girl's door
to send her home, but they have the wrong one!
Find her door. (Hint: It's the one that is different.)

ANSWER: 4.

Sulley calls the girl Boo. Mike is angry. He can't
believe Sulley has given the girl a name!

Boo has disappeared. Sulley runs to look for her.

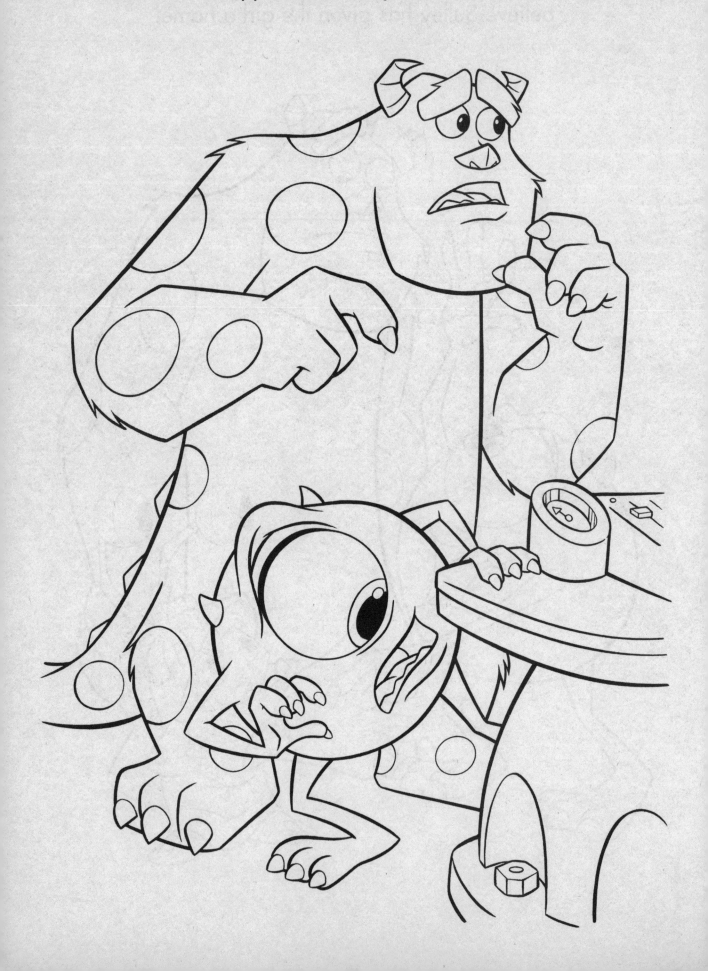

Mike meets someone who says he has a plan to get rid of Boo. Have a grown-up help you cut out each puzzle piece. Put the puzzle together to find out who has the plan. Tape the pieces together on the back. Then color them.

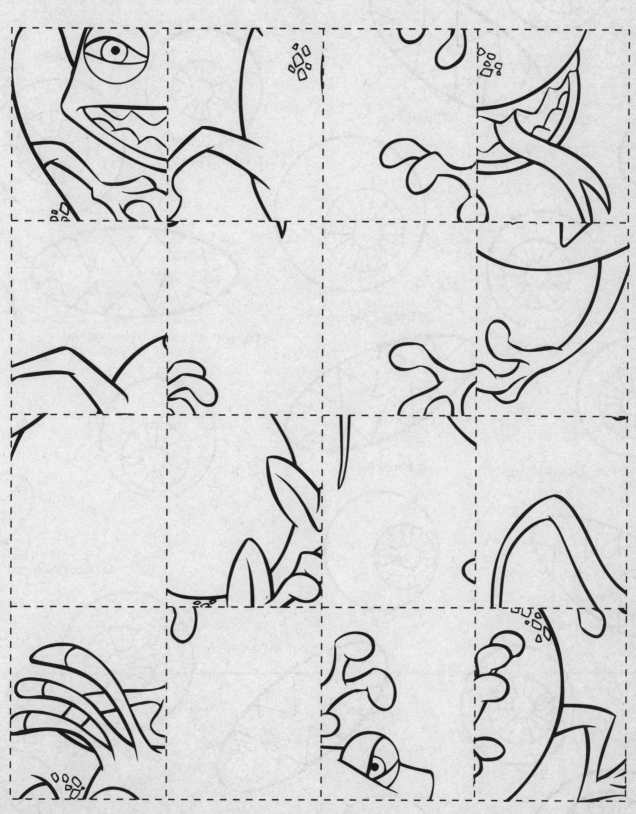

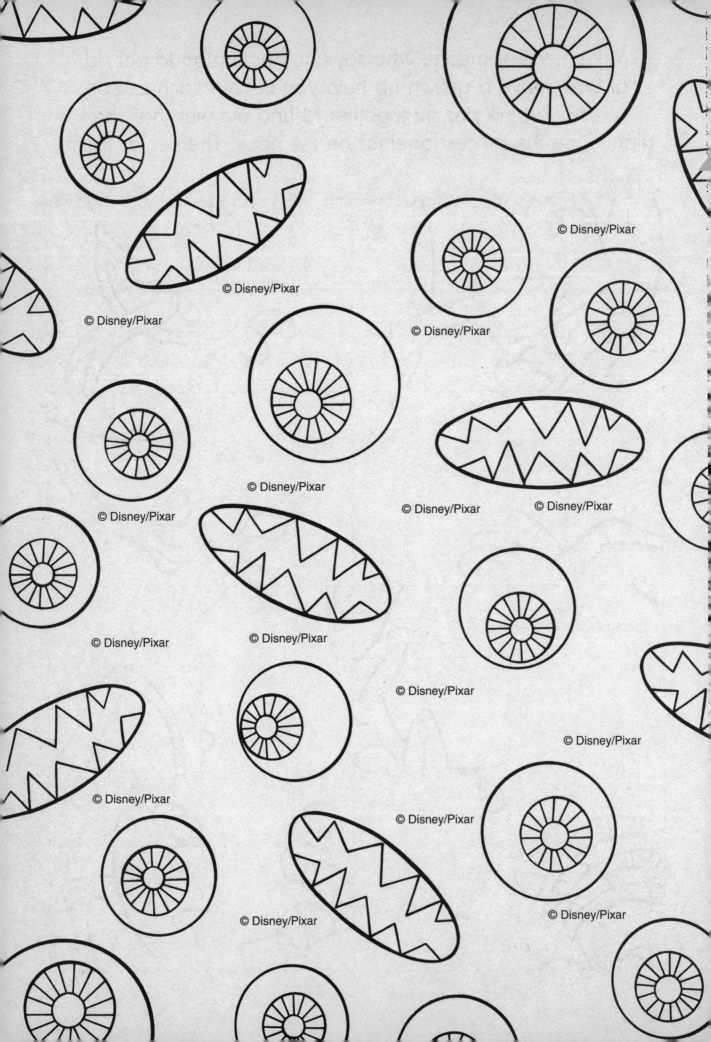

Sulley thinks Boo is gone forever.

Sulley hears Boo's voice! Which monster is she?

Sulley is glad that Boo is safe.

Mike catches up with Sulley and Boo
and tells them to follow him.
To find out where he takes them,
close one eye and tilt the top of
the page away from you.

Randall has put Boo's door back. Sulley doesn't trust Randall, so Mike walks right into Boo's room to prove that everything is safe.

Oh, no!

Randall sets a trap for
Boo, but he catches Mike by mistake.

Randall is surprised to see Mike in the box.

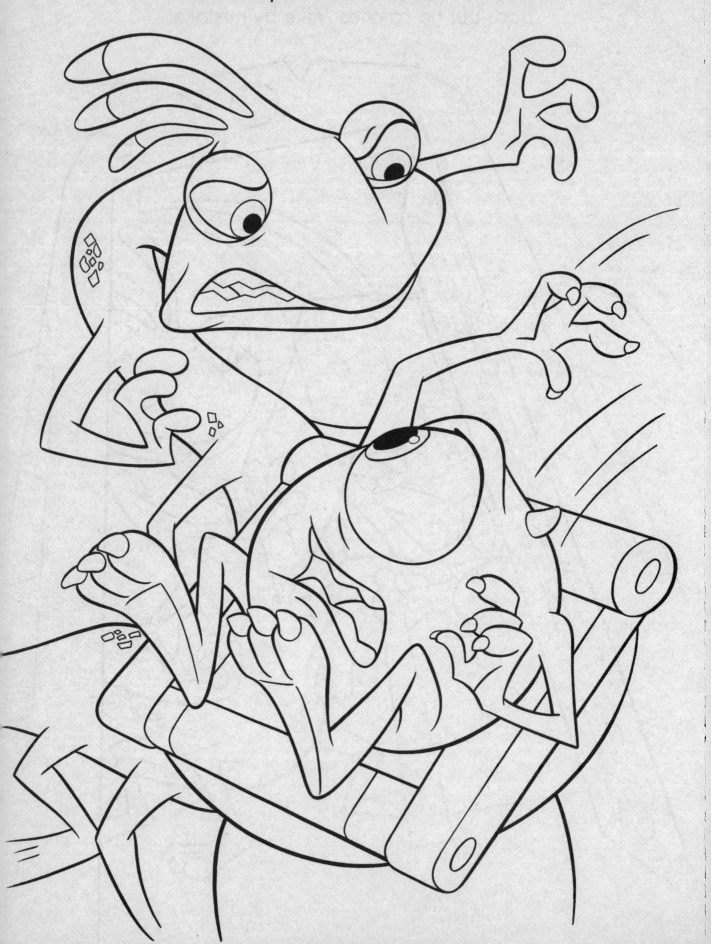

Boo finds a secret door that leads to Randall's hideout!

Sulley and Boo find Mike. They all run away
from Randall. He has a scream machine!

Sulley wants to tell Waternoose what has happened. The boss won't listen. Waternoose asks Sulley to teach the new Scarers how to roar.

Sulley's roar scares Boo.

Who is Waternoose surprised to see? To find out, unscramble the words below and write the letters on the blanks. Then write each boxed letter in order on the blanks below.

LABL [ ] ___ ___ ___

KOBO ___ [ ] ___ ___

ROGF ___ ___ [ ] ___

ANSWER: ___ ___ ___

ANSWER: Boo.

Waternoose is mad because Sulley and Mike have brought a kid into the monster world.

Waternoose and Randall grab Boo, and they send Sulley and Mike into the human world.

Mike thinks they'll never get home.

Mike is mad at Sulley. He throws a snowball at him.

Mike and Sulley make a new friend,
who tells them that there is a town nearby.

Sulley has an idea. Connect the dots to find out what he builds.

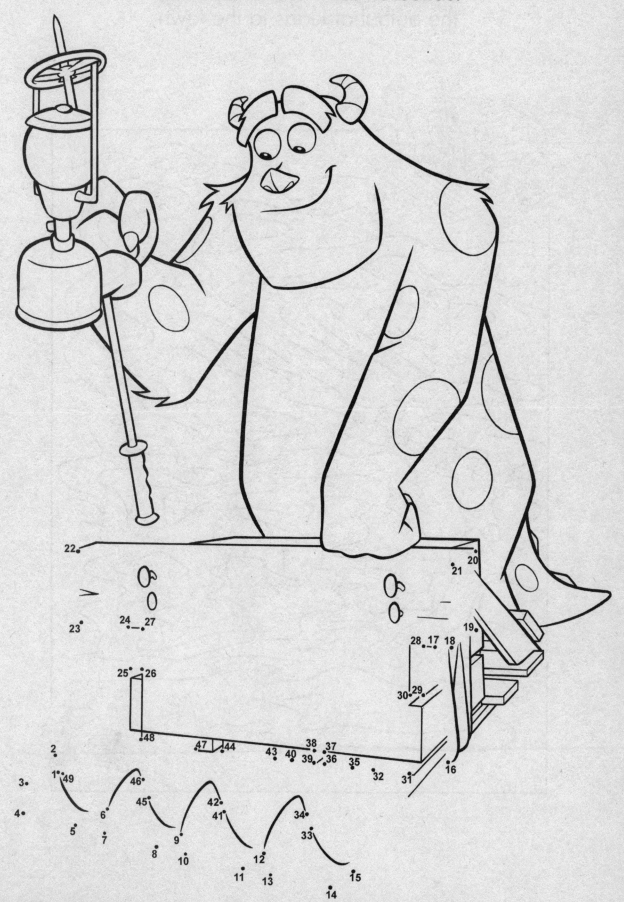

Sulley knows that if he can get to a town, he can go back to the monster world through a kid's closet door. Help him find the path that leads to the town.

START

FINISH

Sulley finds a town—and a kid's door!

Sulley rescues Boo!

Waternoose and Randall want to stop Sulley!

Mike catches up with Sulley. He can't tell that Randall has made himself invisible and is hitting his friend!

Mike, Sulley, and Boo run away from Randall.

Celia helps Mike by playing a trick on Randall.
How many Cs can you find hidden on this page?

Randall gets mixed up! Can you find everything that begins with the letter W?

ANSWER: Mike, milk, mitt, monsters, mop, and muffin.

Mike and Sulley want to get Boo back to her door.
But Randall is hot on their trail!

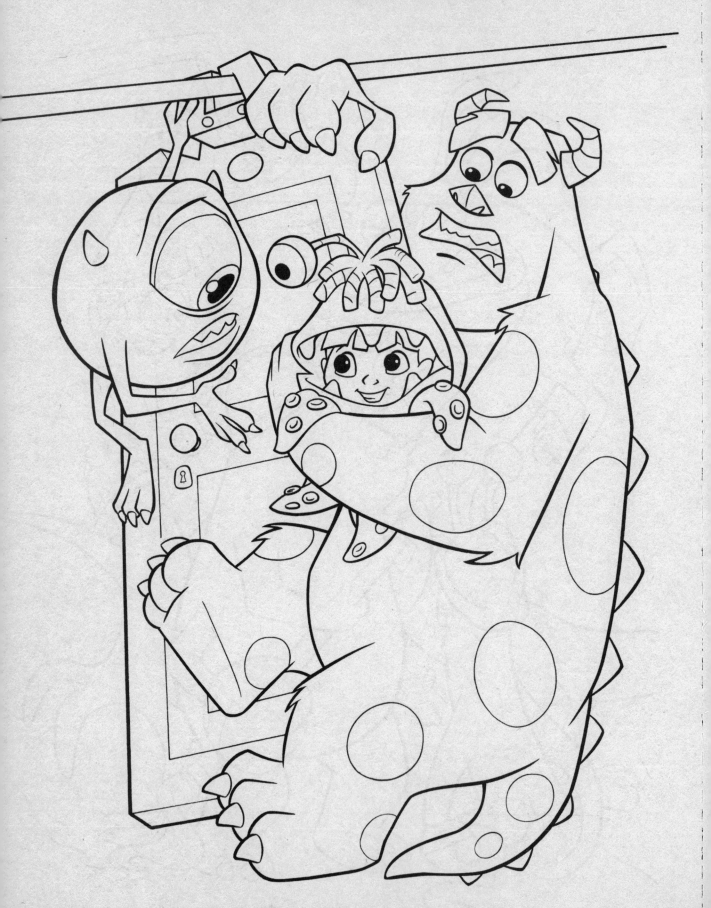

How many doors can you count on this page?

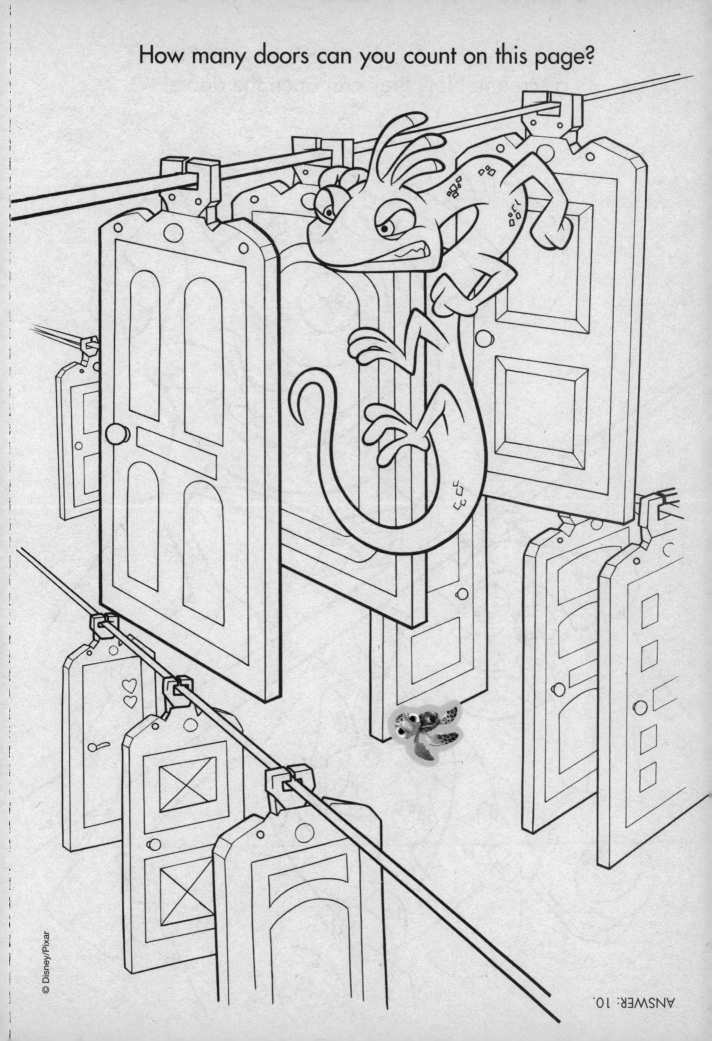

ANSWER: 10.

Boo laughs. Her laugh is more powerful than a scream. Now they can open the doors!

Boo isn't afraid of Randall anymore.
Sulley and Mike send him into the human world.

Uh-oh! Waternoose brings Boo's
door back to the Scare Floor.

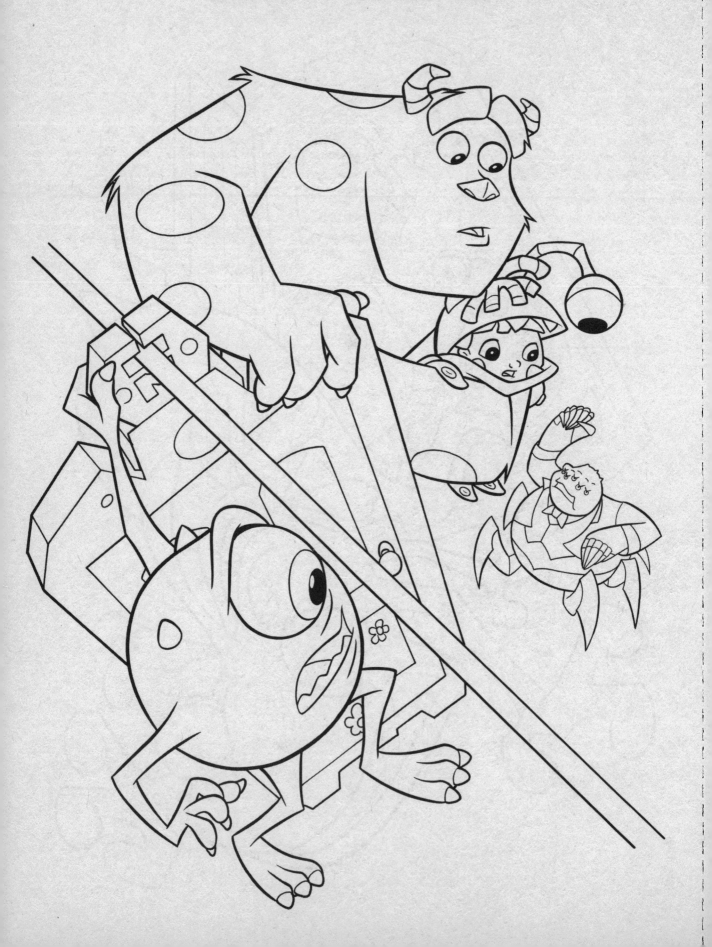

Waternoose has chased Sulley and Boo into a room.
Waternoose tells Sulley his plan to get more
screams. To find out his plan, begin at the center
and write the letters on the blanks below
in the order they appear around the spiral.

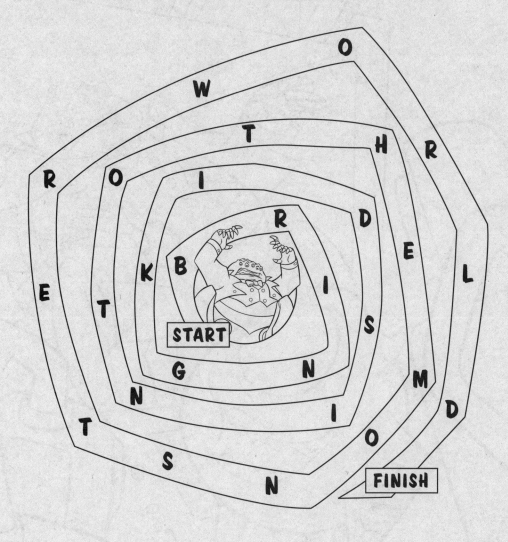

___ ___ ___ ___ ___   ___ ___ ___ ___

___ ___ ___ ___   ___ ___ ___

___ ___ ___ ___ ___   ___ ___ ___ ___

___ ___ ___ ___ ___

ANSWER: Bring kids into the monster world.

Mike and the CDA heard what
Waternoose said. He's in big trouble now!

Have a grown-up help you cut out each puzzle piece.
Put the puzzle together to find out who is CDA Agent Number
One. Tape the pieces together. Then color them.

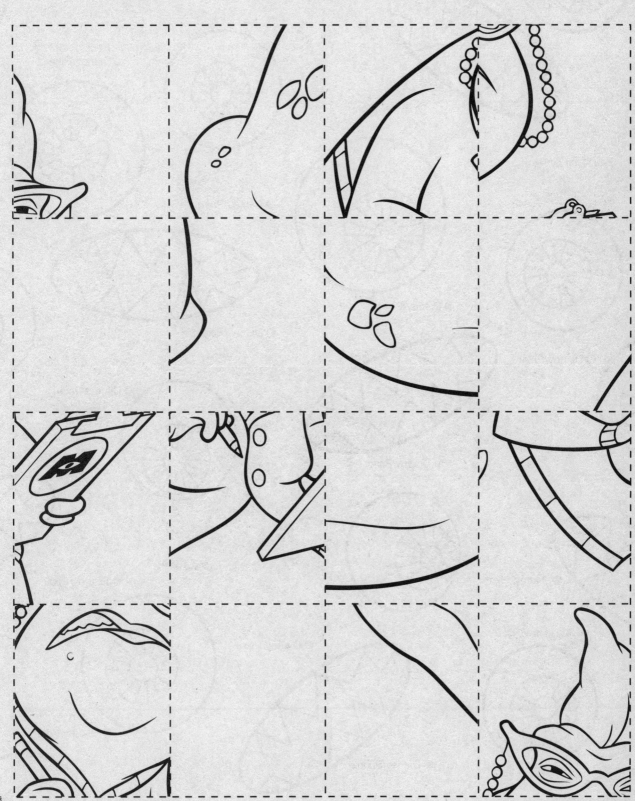

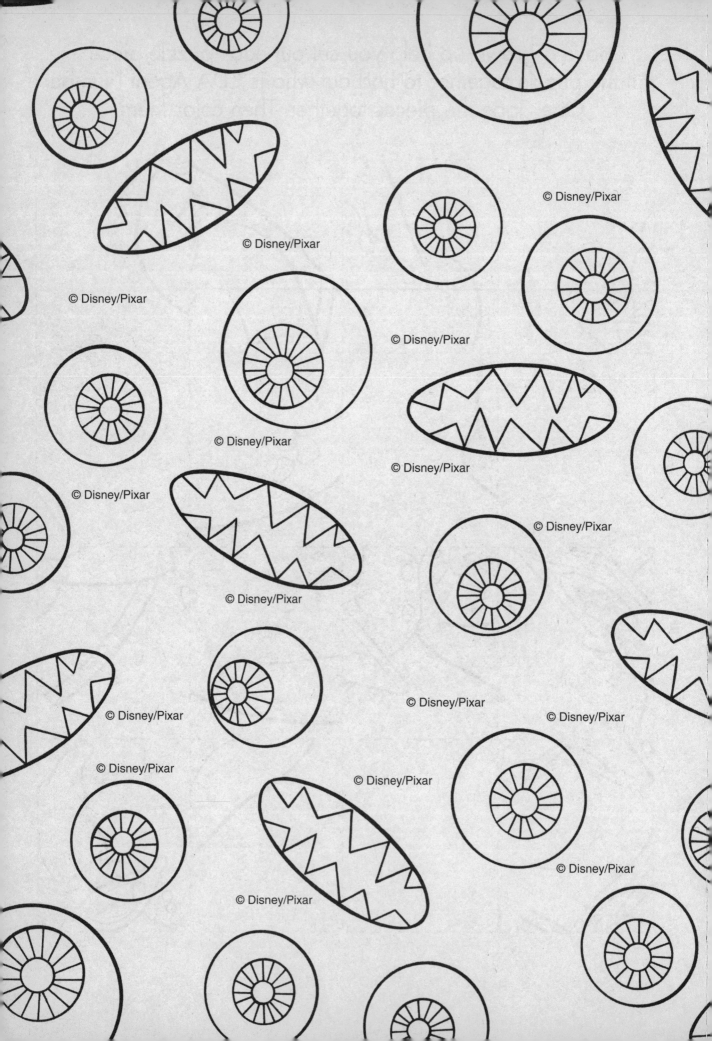

Waternoose is taken away—for good!

Now it's time for Boo to go home.
Sulley must say goodbye to her.

Boo is finally home in her own room.
Find everything that begins with *B*.

ANSWER: Ball, basket, bed, blanket, blocks, Boo, books, and brush.

Thanks to Boo, Sulley has learned that children's laughs make even more energy than their screams. Now he's the boss at Monsters, Inc. He shows monsters how to make kids laugh.

Mike has a surprise for Sulley. It's Boo's door!

"Kitty!" Boo says. Sulley and Boo are together again!

It's Nemo's first day of school. He is so excited!

Nemo has a weak fin.
Marlin thinks the ocean is not safe for his son.

Nemo meets some kids at school. Follow the line from each classmate to his or her name.

TAD   PEARL   SHELDON

Mr. Ray, their teacher, is taking the kids on a field trip.
Marlin asks Mr. Ray to keep an eye on Nemo.

Nemo and his friends see a boat.

Marlin has followed Nemo to make sure he is safe.

Nemo wants to tag the fishing boat to prove that he is brave.
Help him by finding a safe path through the maze.

Nemo touches the boat, but then a diver catches him!

Marlin asks some fish if they have seen the boat that took Nemo, but nobody will talk to him!

A fish named Dory has seen a boat.
She tells Marlin to follow her!

Dory swims very fast. Marlin is afraid he will
lose her. How many other fish can you count?

Dory has a bad memory!
She asks Marlin why he is following her.

Marlin and Dory meet a shark named
Bruce, who invites them to a party.

The party is for sharks who are trying to stop eating fish. Marlin meets a new "chum" there.

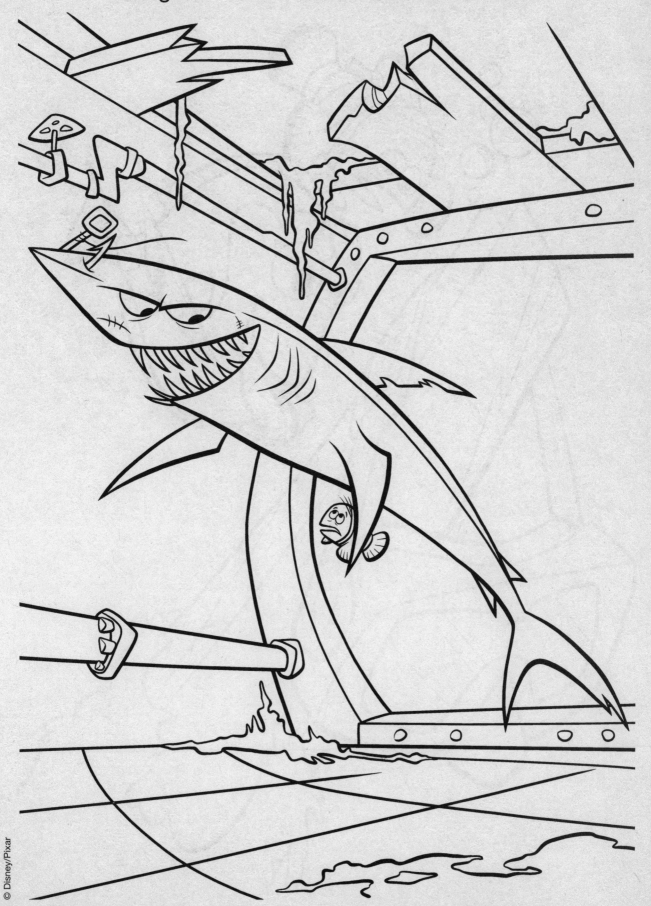

Marlin finds a mask that belongs to the diver who took Nemo.
Dory asks the sharks if they can read the writing on it.

But all Bruce wants to do is eat Marlin and Dory.
They escape while the other sharks try to stop Bruce.

Nemo has been taken out of the ocean.
He is now in a fish tank in a dentist's office.

Nemo tells the other fish he is from the ocean.

Nigel, a pelican, visits his fish-tank friends.

Nemo learns he will be a present for the dentist's niece Darla.
Gill, the leader of the tank, has an idea.

There are lots of fish in the tank.

Draw a fish on this page.

Meanwhile, back in the ocean, Dory has dropped the mask!

Dory remembers that she can read. Use the code to read the writing on the mask.

Gill makes Nemo an official member
of the tank and explains the plan to escape.

Back in the ocean, Marlin tells Dory that he wants to look for Nemo by himself.

But Marlin really needs help. Dory asks
some nearby fish for directions to Sydney.

When they come to a trench, Dory wants to swim through it,
but Marlin tricks her into following him over it.

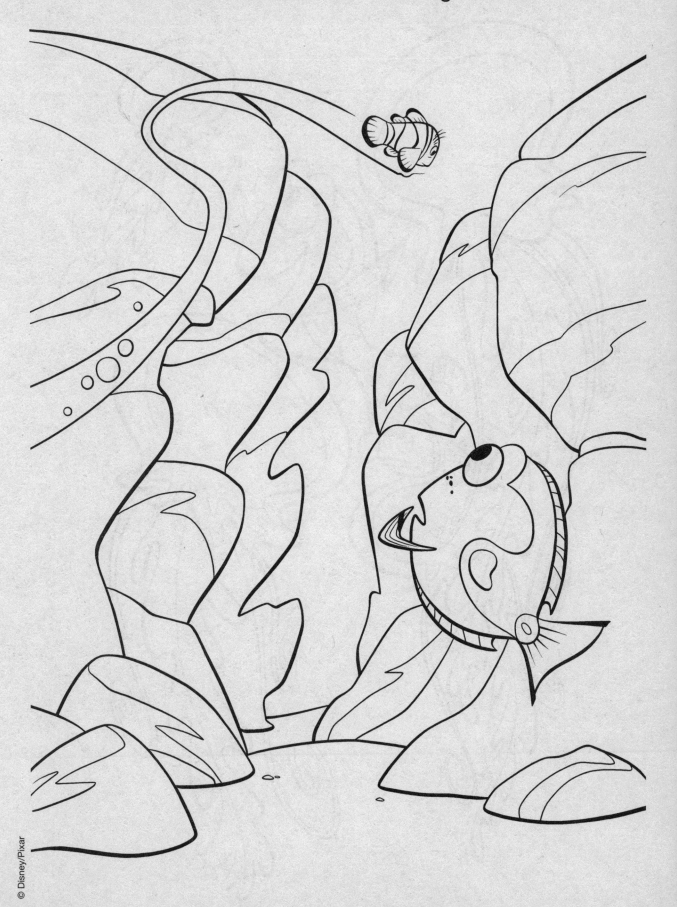

At the top of the trench, Marlin and Dory
are surrounded by jellyfish!

Marlin rescues Dory from the jellyfish.

Gill has a weak fin, just like Nemo!
He teaches Nemo how to be a strong swimmer.

Part of the escape plan is to put a pebble in the filter and let the tank get dirty. Then the dentist will need to take the gang out of the tank to clean it.

The pebble falls out. The fish try to save Nemo.

Nemo is saved!

Marlin catches a ride. He tells his story, and the news about Nemo spreads across the ocean!

Dory plays hide-and-seek with the turtles.
How many baby turtles can you count?

ANSWER: 8.

Nigel hears that Marlin is looking for Nemo.

Nemo learns that his dad is coming to rescue him. He can't believe it!

Nemo is ready to try the plan again. Help him put the pebble in the filter so that the tank gang can escape.

Dory asks a whale for directions to Sydney.
The whale ends up swallowing Dory and Marlin!

Gill's plan is working—the tank gets dirty in no time!
Nemo is covered in algae!

Inside the whale's mouth, Dory and Marlin hang on to his tongue. They don't want to be swallowed!

The whale spouts Marlin and Dory into Sydney Harbor.

The next day, the tank gang wakes up
to a new filter—and a clean tank.

The dentist puts Nemo into a bag. Nemo tries
to roll away, but the dentist catches him.

Marlin and Dory have been searching all
night for Nemo, but it's a big harbor!

Oh, no! A pelican wants to eat Dory and Marlin.

It's Darla's birthday. She is ready for her present—Nemo!

Nemo plays dead, hoping the dentist will flush him down the toilet and free him. But the dentist takes him to the trash can instead!

Marlin thinks he has arrived too late. Look at this page
for sixty seconds. Then turn the page and see
if you can find four differences.

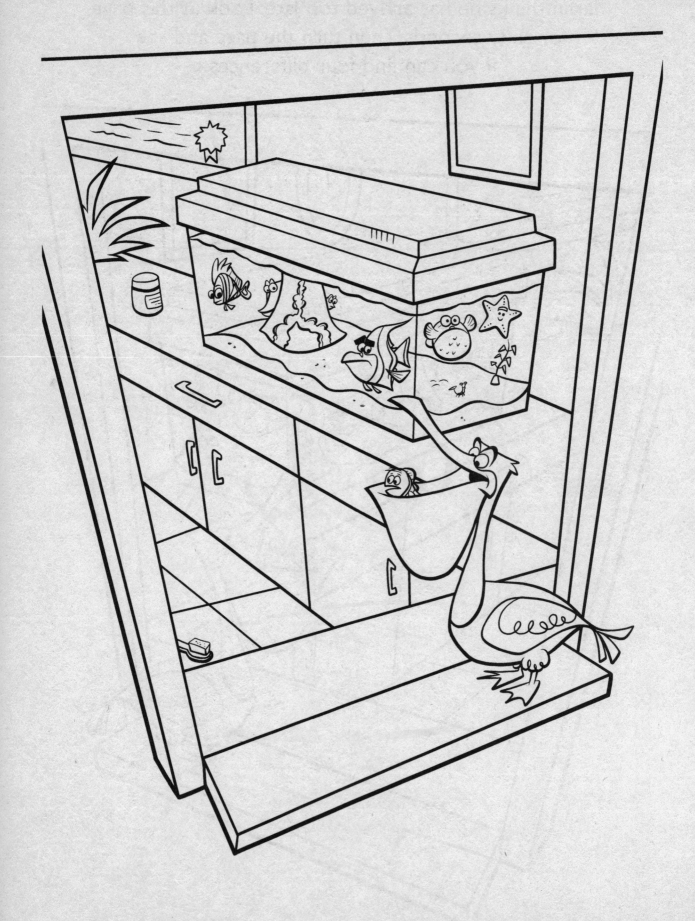

ANSWER: On this page, the clock is missing from the wall, there is fish food on the counter, Dory is missing, and there's a toothbrush on the floor.

Nemo's bag breaks! Soon he won't be able to breathe.

Gill flips Nemo into the spit sink, and Nemo goes
down the drain and into the ocean. He's back
in the water and can breathe again!

Marlin tells Dory they were too late
and he must leave by himself.

Dory meets Nemo at last—
but she can't remember who he is!

Marlin finds Dory and Nemo! But then
Dory is caught in a net full of fish.

Nemo tells Marlin he has an idea.
What does he want the fish to do? Use the code to find out!

O = ◆

D = ●   M = ☐   S = ◎

I = ★   N = ♣   W = ♥

It works! The net breaks, and all the fish escape.

Marlin and Nemo are finally back together!

Nemo and Marlin return home. And from now on, Nemo will always listen to his father.

Freedom!

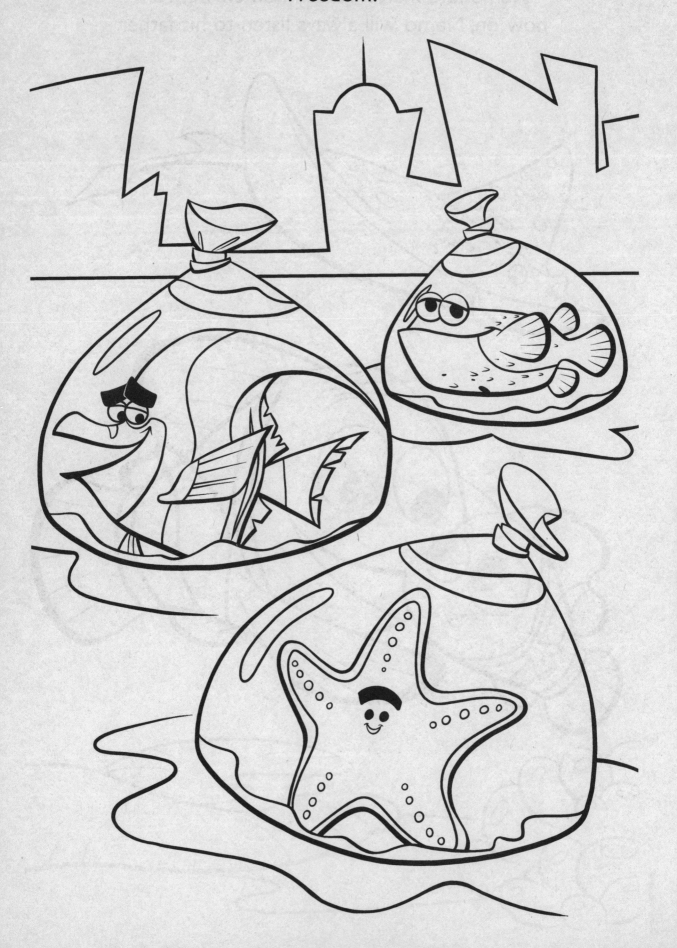

DISNEP PRESENTS A PIXAR FILM

THE INCREDIBLES

Mr. Incredible is the number-one Super!

Mr. Incredible is always ready
to battle evil in the world.

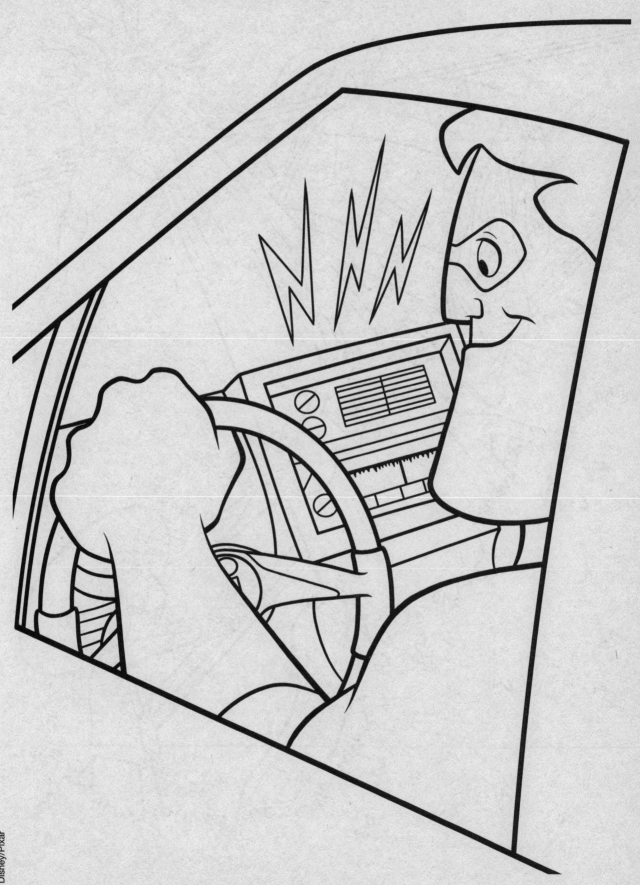

No job is too big or too small for Mr. Incredible.

Mr. Incredible's biggest fan, Buddy, wants to help his hero. To find out what Mr. Incredible tells him, close one eye and tilt the top of the page away from you.

ANSWER: I work alone!

Elastigirl beats Mr. Incredible to the punch! But there's something she thinks he needs to be. To find out what it is, circle every third letter. Then write the circled letters in order on the blanks.

DCFGALRHEBQXTMIBUBNSLJPE

__ __ __ __ __ __ __ __ __!

Frozone is Mr. Incredible's best friend.

Buddy takes Mr. Incredible on a wild ride
when he tries to use his new jet boots!

There's still more hero work to do before the day is done.
Mr. Incredible saves a train full of people!

Help Mr. Incredible get to his wedding on time.

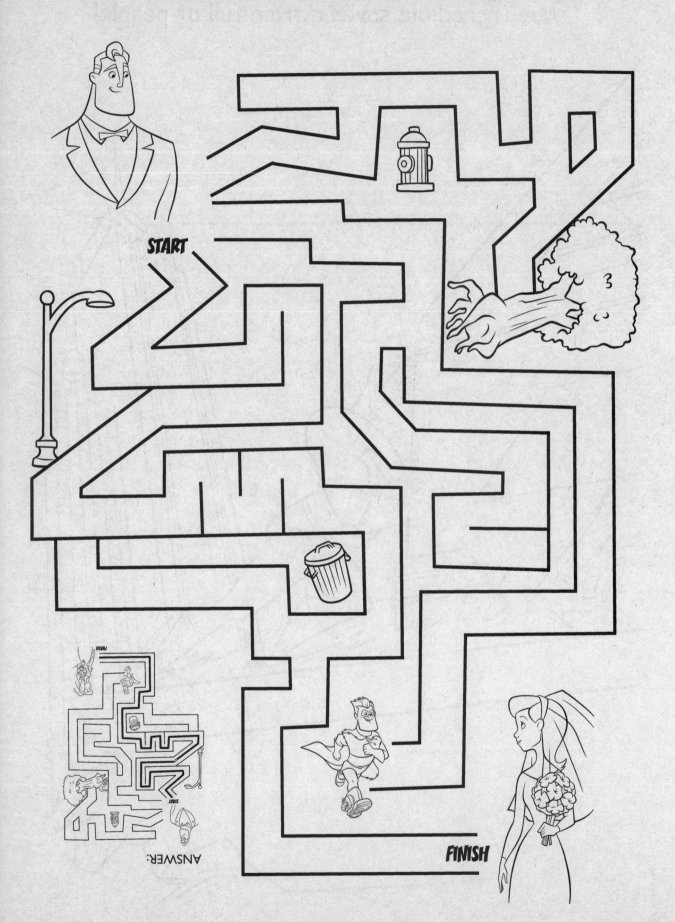

START

FINISH

ANSWER:

Some people don't want to be saved. They think the Supers cause more harm than good! Hold this page up to a mirror to see what the newspaper headlines say.

ANSWER: Supers Sued! Jumper Seeks Damages!

Mr. Incredible is forced to live in secret
as the not-so-incredible Bob Parr.

Sometimes Bob forgets to act like a normal guy.

Everyone in Bob's family has Super powers
except the baby, Jack-Jack. He's just good
at making a super mess at suppertime!

Bob's wife, Helen, used to be known as Elastigirl. Her Super-elastic arms come in handy when she's trying to stop fights between Super-fast Dash and his sister, Violet, who can turn invisible and create force fields.

Frozone's new name is Lucius. Lucius is trying to leave his crime-fighting days behind, but Bob can't. Together, they listen to a police scanner.

Just like old times, Bob and Lucius
can still save the day.

The Supers' true identities are their biggest secrets. Find the hero names and secret identities of these Supers. Look forward, backward, up, down, and diagonally.

SUPER NAMES	SECRET IDENTITY
Mr. Incredible	Bob Parr
Elastigirl	Helen Parr
Frozone	Lucius Best

```
M R I N C R E D I B L E
T V O D E X O S R D B U
E E R O I R T M O R K E
N W B O B P A R R E P L
O C U X L A U A O I G A
Z L D F Y R P E N K A S
O R A V E N H K O E F T
R V O D E E O S R D K I
F C U L L A U T O Z H G
T S E B S U I C U L O I
B H A V E L H K O N X R
A U A O I C U X L V D L
```

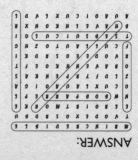

ANSWER:

A mysterious woman named Mirage works for an old fan of Mr. Incredible. She has a secret message for Bob.

Bob's boss, Mr. Huph,
is not happy with Bob's work.

Bob gets frustrated with Mr. Huph.

Luckily, Mirage offers Bob a job.
He'll work as Mr. Incredible to stop
the Omnidroid, a learning robot.

Mirage takes Bob to Nomanisan Island.

Mirage's jet drops Mr. Incredible on the island,
where he is attacked by the Omnidroid.

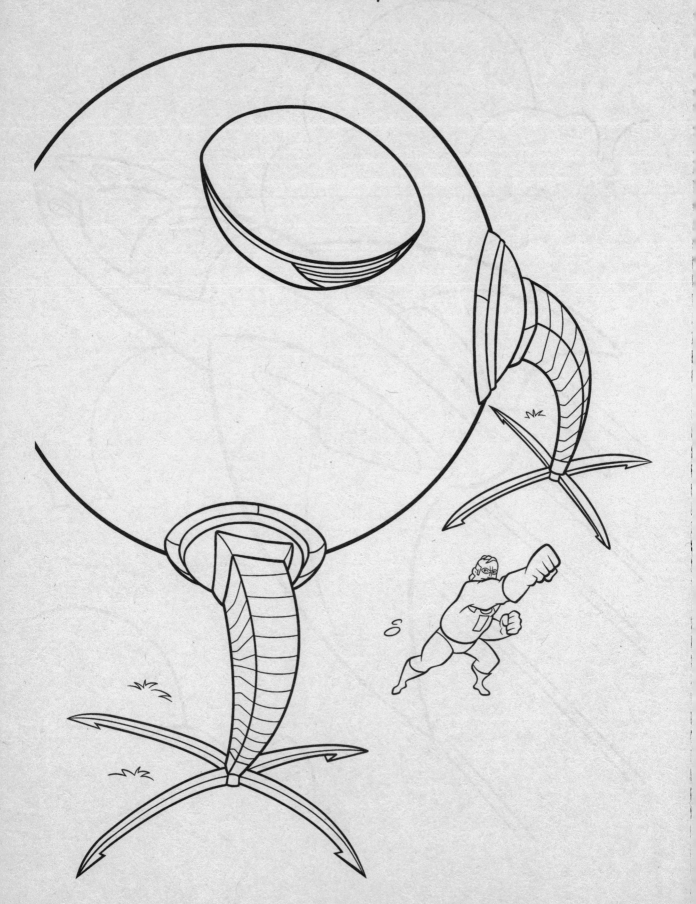

Mr. Incredible fights back and wins!
Mirage and a mysterious man watch him
on a computer screen.

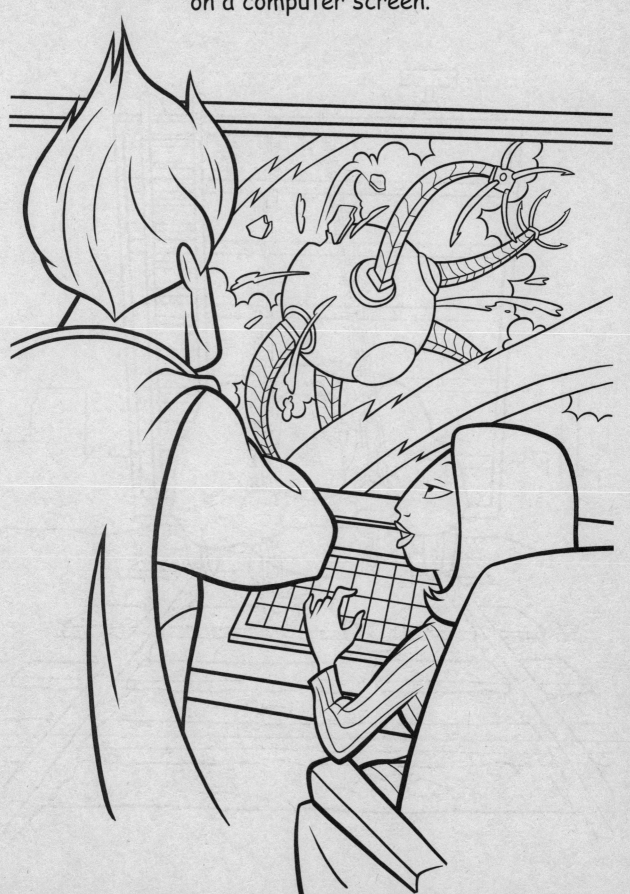

Back home, Bob works out by pulling trains.
He wants to be as strong as he used to be.

Bob needs some extra-special help with his Super suit.
To find out the only person who can do the job, close
one eye and tilt the top of the page away from you.

ANSWER: Edna Mode!

With a new suit ready, Bob takes another assignment. Helen hears Bob on the phone and wonders what he is up to.

Use the code below to find out the name of the evil genius who wants to destroy the Supers.

A	B	C	D	E	F	G	H	I	J	K	L	M	N	O	P	Q	R	S	T	U	V	W	X	Y	Z
1	2	3	4	5	6	7	8	9	10	11	12	13	14	15	16	17	18	19	20	21	22	23	24	25	26

___ ___ ___ ___ ___ ___ ___ ___!
19   25   14   4   18   15   13   5

ANSWER: Syndrome!

Mr. Incredible discovers that he has been working for a villain! The evil Syndrome sends a bigger, smarter Omnidroid to capture Mr. Incredible.

Mr. Incredible makes a daring escape.

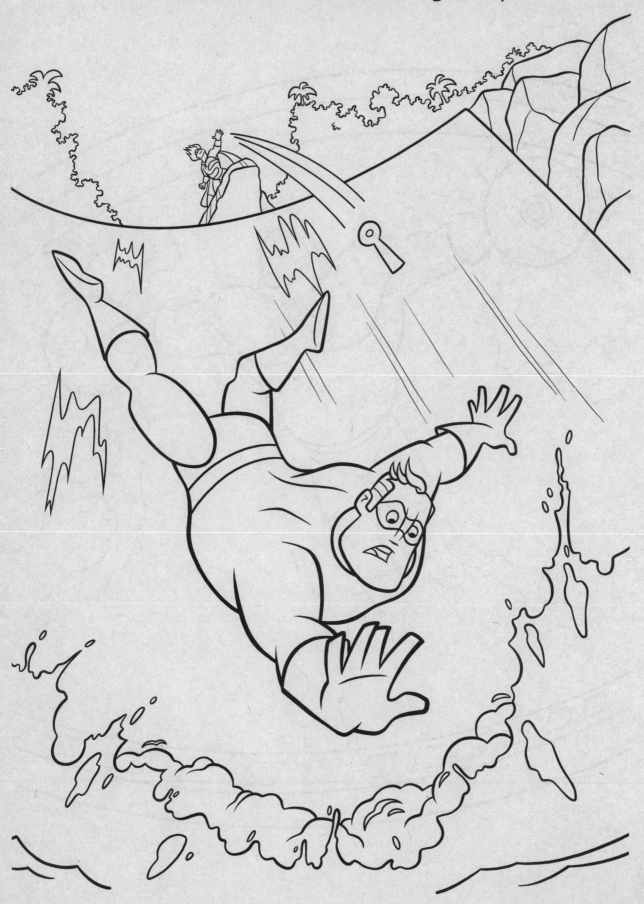

Mr. Incredible is Syndrome's prisoner!

Underwater, Mr. Incredible finds a message from Gazerbeam, a missing Super. Find out what it says by replacing each letter with the one that comes before it in the alphabet.

L S P O P T !

___ ___ ___ ___ ___ ___ !

Syndrome thinks Mr. Incredible
is gone for good! But is he?

Not a chance! Mr. Incredible gets
busy doing what he does best.

Back at home, Helen visits Edna Mode. Edna tells Helen she has designed Super suits for the entire family. She also gives Helen a tracking device for the suits.

Mr. Incredible discovers Syndrome's computer.
Could the password be *Kronos*?

Helen wants to know where Bob is.
She activates the tracking device.

Mr. Incredible's luck has run out!
Syndrome captures him once again.

Helen rushes to find Mr. Incredible. Meanwhile,
the kids discover their new Super suits.

Look out, world! Dash is ready for action.

Helen heads off in her jet
to Nomanisan Island.

Mr. Incredible watches helplessly
as Syndrome attacks Helen's jet.

Elastigirl finds some
unexpected guests on board.

Syndrome's weapons just miss Helen and the kids.

Elastigirl turns into a parachute
to get her kids to safety!

Elastigirl tells Dash and Vi to use their
Super powers if they get into any trouble.
Then she heads out to save Mr. Incredible.

Elastigirl is stretched to her limits
at Syndrome's headquarters.

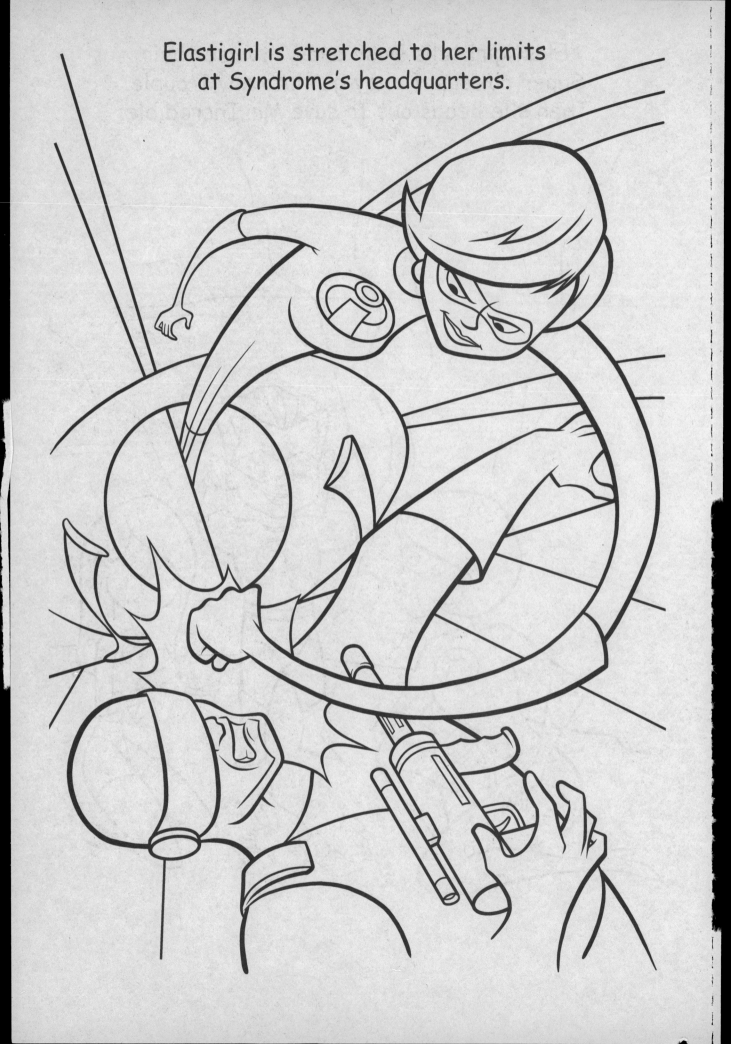

Mr. Incredible is happy to see his wife. But their get-together is cut short when Mirage tells them that Dash and Vi have set off one of Syndrome's alarms.

Mom and Dad to the rescue!

Mr. and Mrs. Incredible show Dash and Vi how it's done!

Oh, no!

Syndrome is always one
step ahead of the Incredible family.

Syndrome reveals his evil plan. When he sends
the Omnidroid to the big city of Metroville,
he will be the only one who knows how to defeat it.
Then he will look like the world's best Super.

Mirage helps the Incredibles escape in a rocket. Guide them to a safe landing so they can save the city from the Omnidroid.

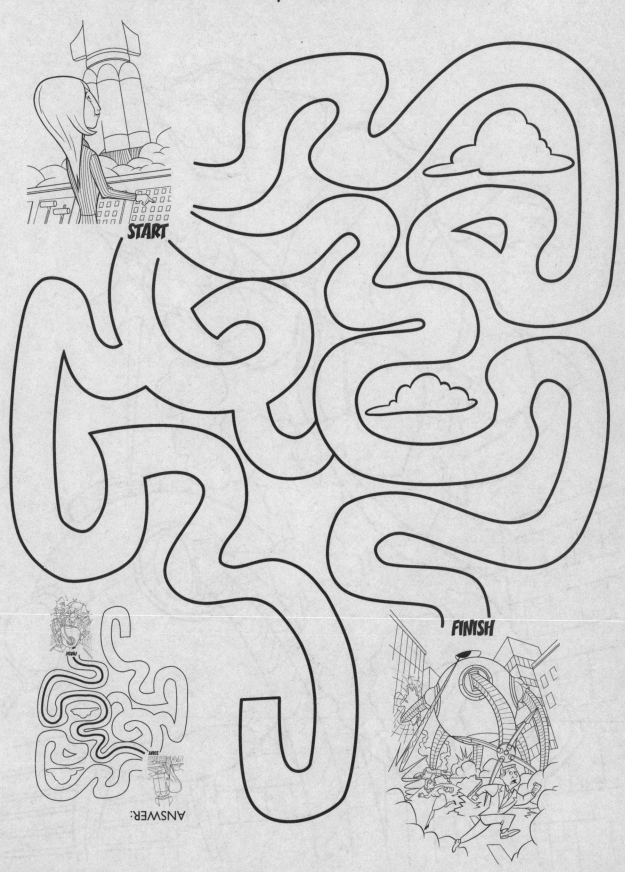

START

FINISH

ANSWER:

Syndrome learns that trying to be
a Super is harder than it looks.

Mr. Incredible's family does not want him
to try to defeat the Omnidroid alone.
They will all work together.

Mr. Incredible throws the Omnidroid's
remote device to Dash.

Teamwork wins as the Supers
save the day once again!

The Supers are back!

Upset at his defeat, Syndrome takes Jack-Jack.
But the baby shows that he is truly an Incredible!

Elastigirl turns into a parachute
to save her littlest Super, Jack-Jack.

It's back to normal for the Parr family.

It's time to be Super again!

Lightning McQueen wants to be the first rookie
to win the Piston Cup!

Lightning McQueen is all about speed. How many times can you find the word SPEED in the puzzle below? (Look backward, forward, and down.)

ANSWER: 6.

On the way to a race, Lightning accidentally
rolls out of his trailer!

Lightning gets lost and ends up destroying a road
in a town called Radiator Springs.

Lightning is locked up!

To learn the name of this friendly tow truck, replace each letter with the one that comes before it in the alphabet.

N B U F S

_ _ _ _ _

ANSWER: Mater.

Lightning must use Bessie to fix the road.
Use the key below to find out what Bessie is.

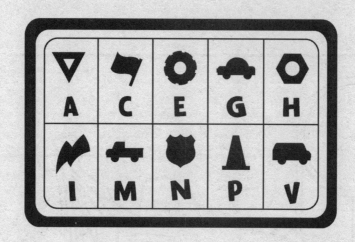

Flo's V8 Café serves up the freshest oil and fuel in Radiator Springs.

Luigi runs the local tire shop.

Nobody changes tires faster than Guido.

Finally, Lightning has finished fixing the road.

Mater and Sally enjoy the new road.

Mater wants to show Lightning how to tip tractors.
Help Lightning find the path that leads to the tractor so he can join the fun.

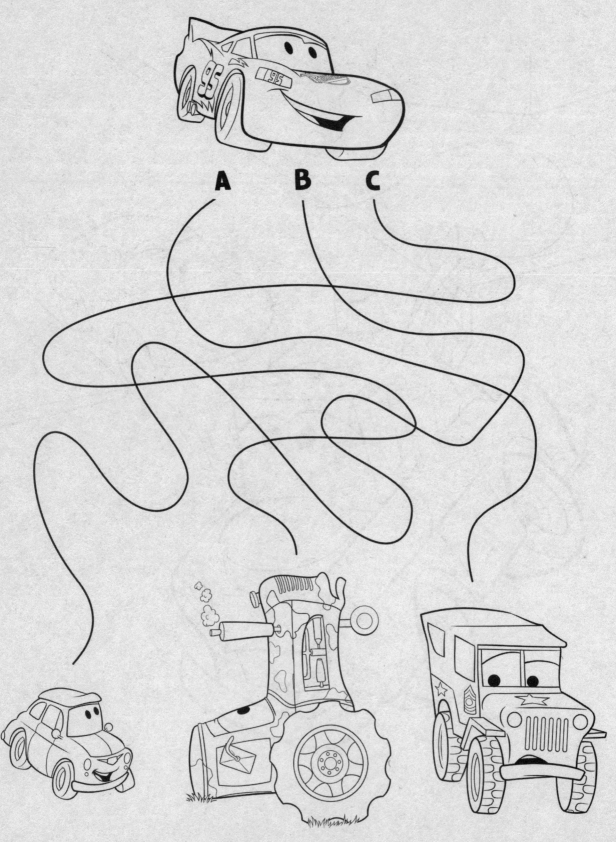

A   B   C

Lightning and Sally enjoy the view of Radiator Springs from above.

Lightning buys new tires from Luigi and Guido.
How many tires are in the pile?

Things look different around Radiator Springs since Lightning came to town.
Study this picture carefully, then try to find six differences on the next page.

Lightning has been found in Radiator Springs!
He tells Sally that he has to leave to get ready for the big race.

During the race, Lightning can't stop thinking about his new friends.
He misses them.

Lightning's friends from Radiator Springs have come to the race!
Match each car to its shadow.

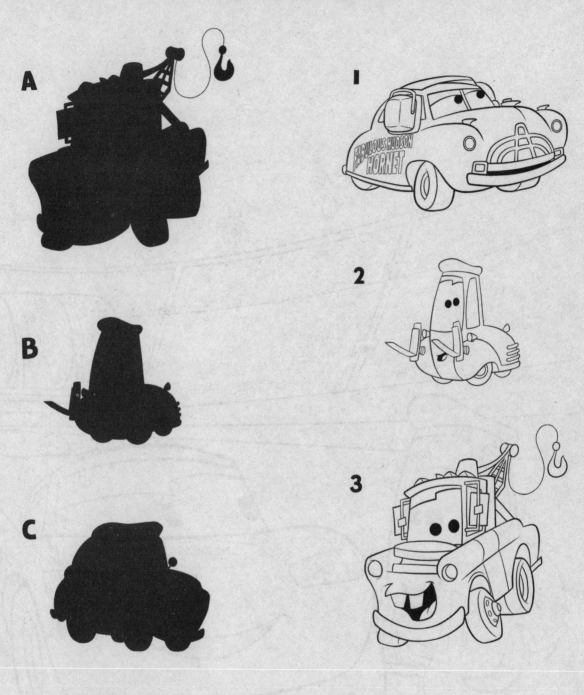

A

B

C

D

1

2

3

4

Lightning gets a flat tire!
Luckily, Guido is there to change it in record time!

Instead of trying to win the race, Lightning stops
to help The King cross the finish line.

Sally is happy when Lightning returns to Radiator Springs
to open his new racing headquarters.

Mater and Lightning fly to Japan for the first World Grand Prix race.

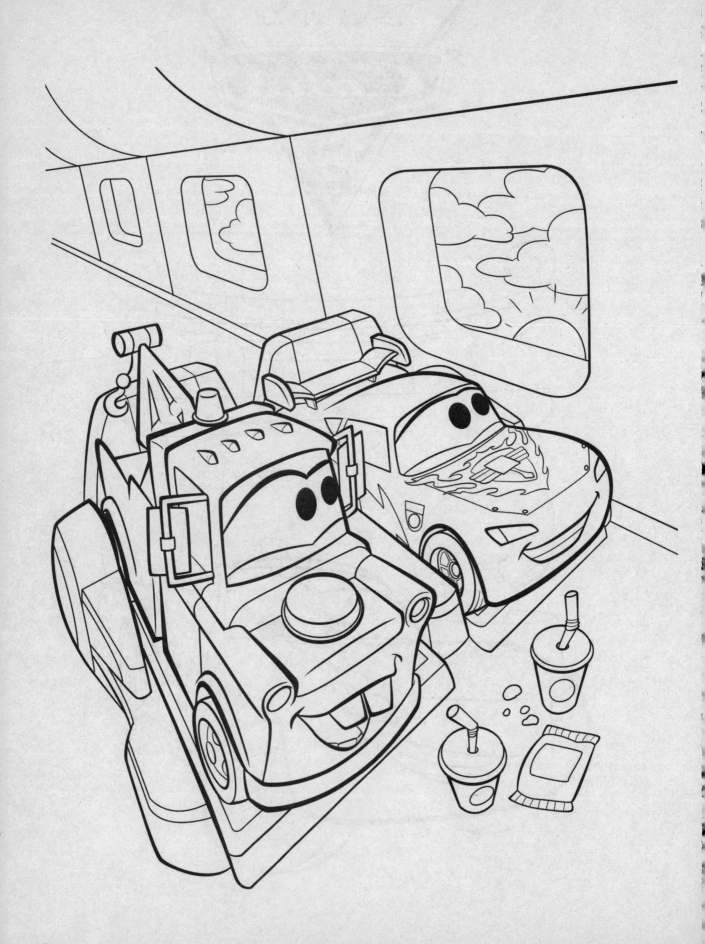

Finn McMissile is a secret agent.

Unscramble the letters below to find out the name of this secret agent.

L H Y E O L

H _ _ _ _ _

Holley thinks Mater is a secret agent.

Team Lightning McQueen gets ready for the first race!

During the race, Holley talks to Mater on his headset.

Lightning loses the race to Francesco, his biggest rival.

Mater decides to go back to Radiator Springs.

Acer and Grem work for the evil Professor Z. They're following Mater!

Acer chases Finn and Mater!

Mater and his friends enjoy the sights and sounds of Paris.

Team Lightning McQueen travels to the next World Grand Prix race.
What country are they in? To find out, circle every third letter.
Then write those letters in order on the blanks.

DAIWETCUAPFLXOY

_____ _____ _____ _____ _____

ANSWER: Italy.

Guido and Luigi are happy to be back in their home country.
Circle the two pictures of Guido and Luigi that are exactly alike.

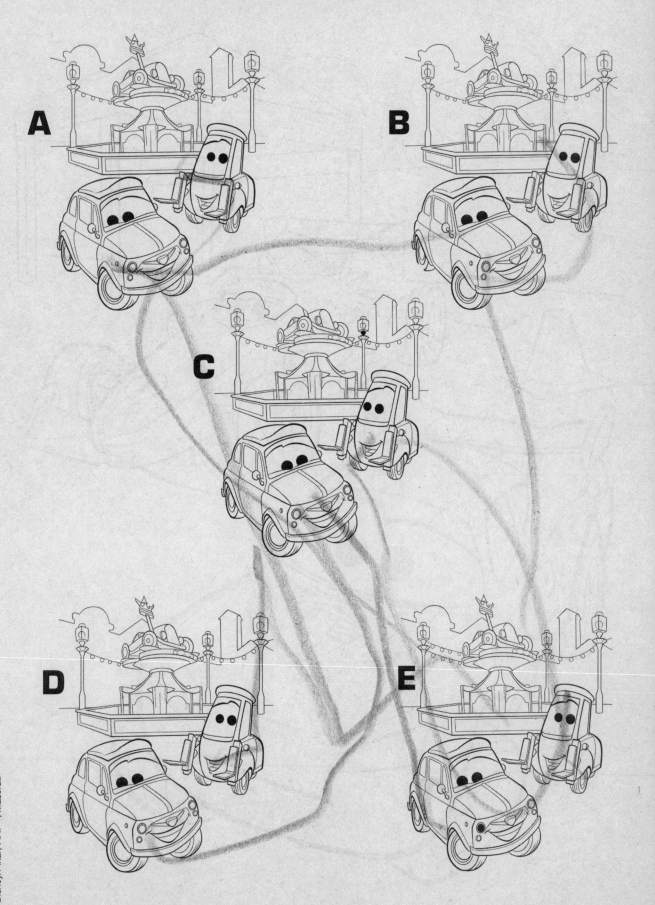

ANSWER: A and D.

Francesco is confident that he will win the next race.

Carla passes Lightning on the outside!

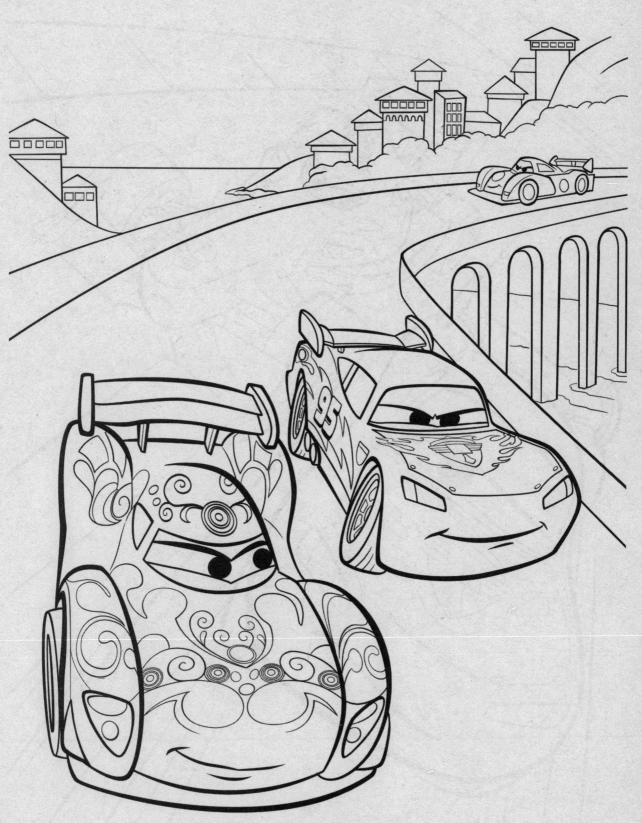

Lightning and Francesco both want to win.

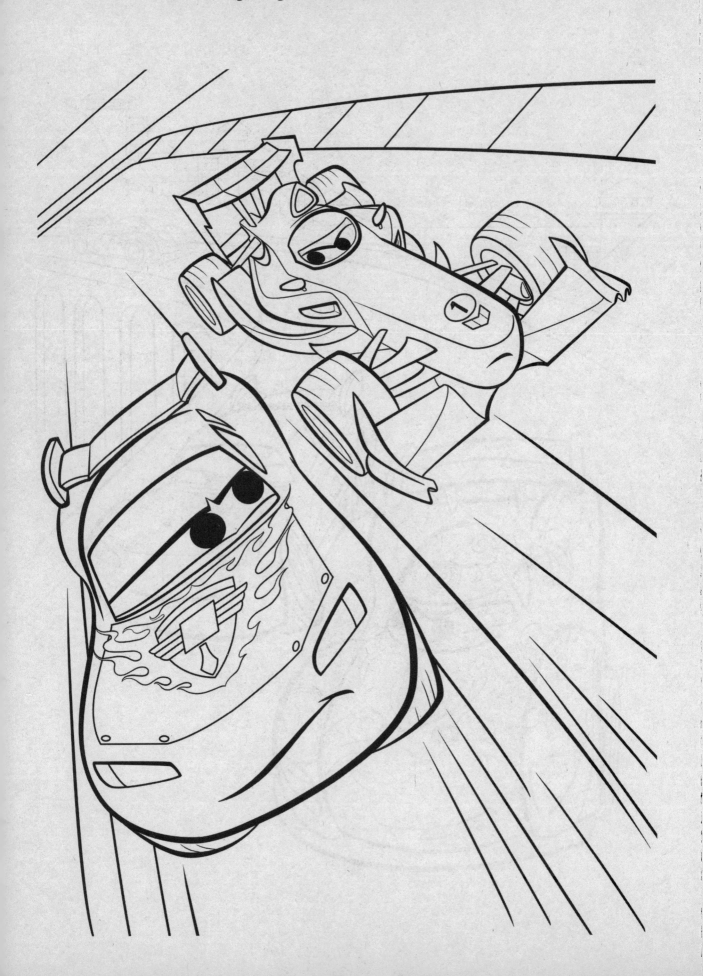

Lightning wins the second race!

Team Lightning McQueen arrives in England!

Mater saves the day by telling the Queen about the bad cars.

Mater and Lightning return to Radiator Springs.

Francesco likes Lightning's hometown.

Lightning and Mater will always be fast friends!

Disney · PIXAR

WALL·E

WALL•E is cleaning up Earth while people travel in space.
One day he finds a plant!

A new robot comes to Earth. Her name is EVE.

EVE is amazed by all the things WALL•E has collected.

WALL•E grabs EVE's spaceship and follows her into space. Hold on tight, WALL•E!

WALL•E meets a cleaning robot named M-O.

Scrub, M-O, scrub!

This paint-bot is not working right.

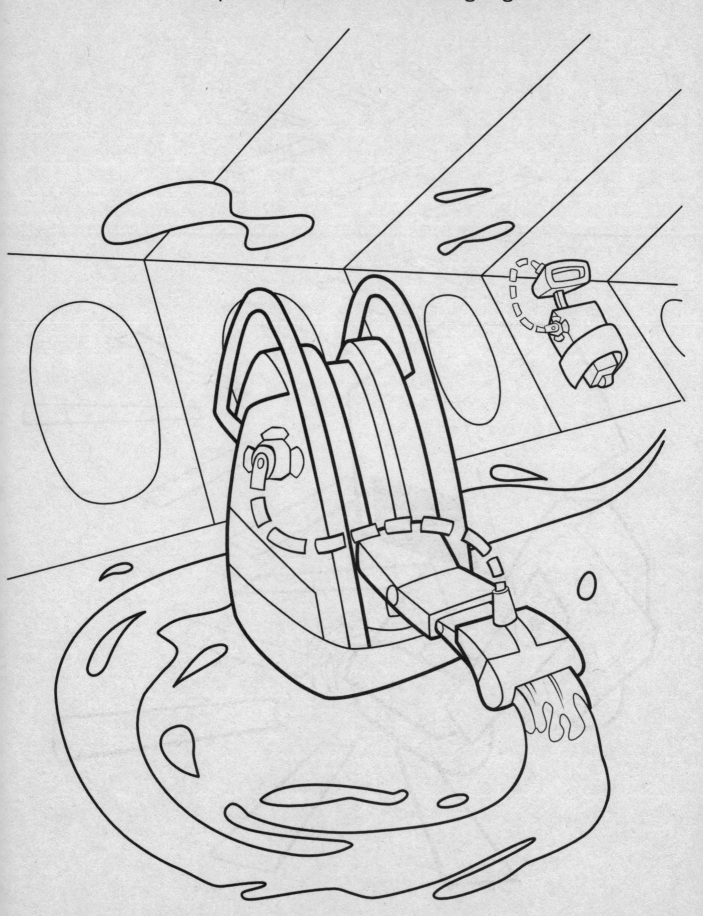

This beautician-bot tries to make WALL•E look pretty.

The reject-bots escape from the repair ward!

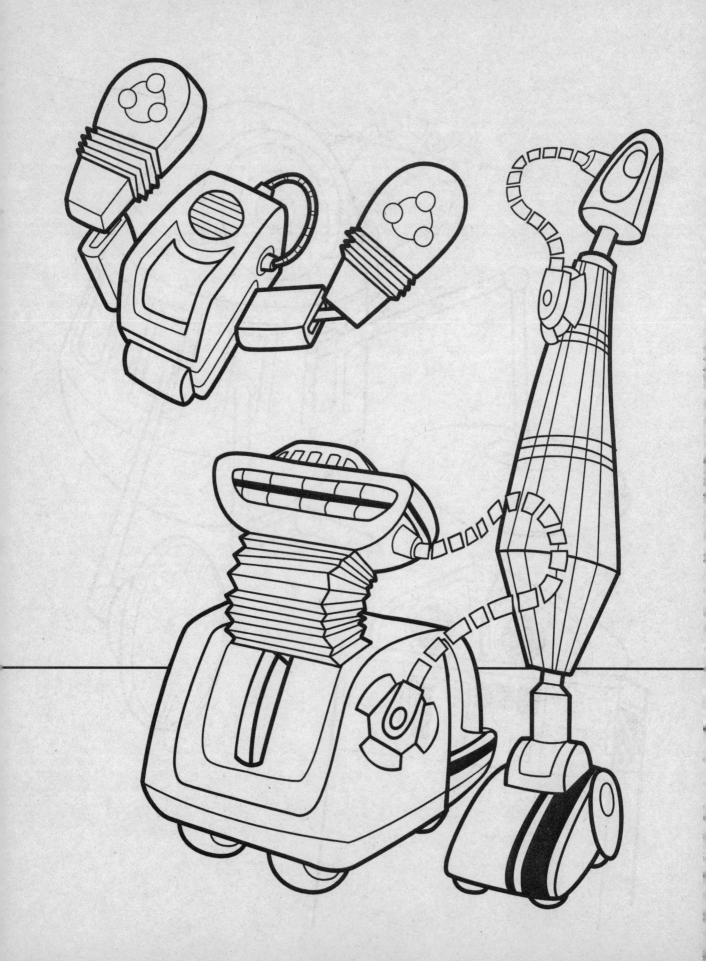

EVE follows the reject-bots.

WALL•E goes for an unexpected ride in space!

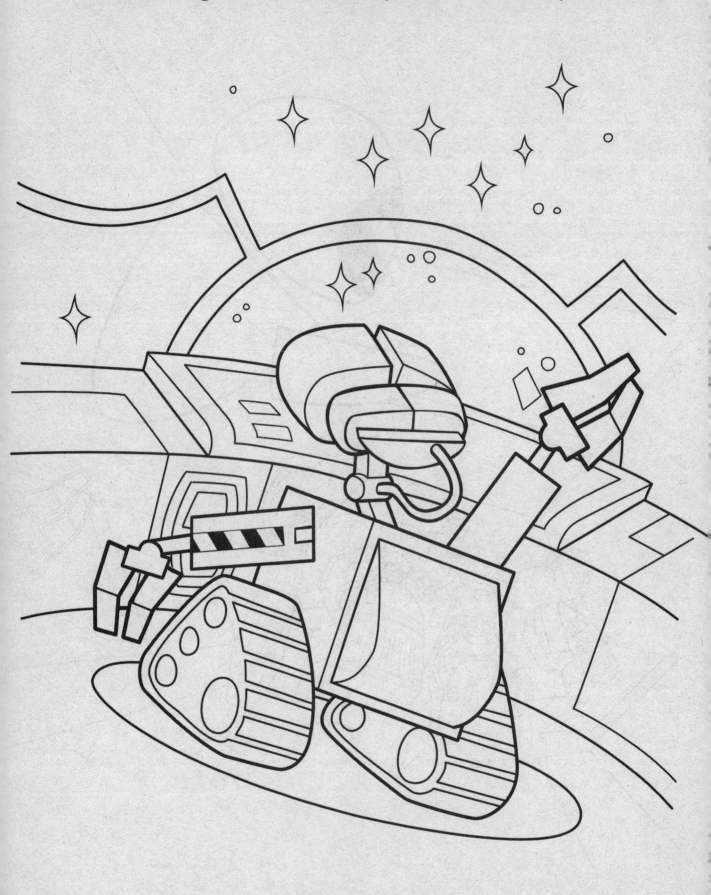

WALL•E and EVE dance among the stars.

This is Auto. He steers the *Axiom*.

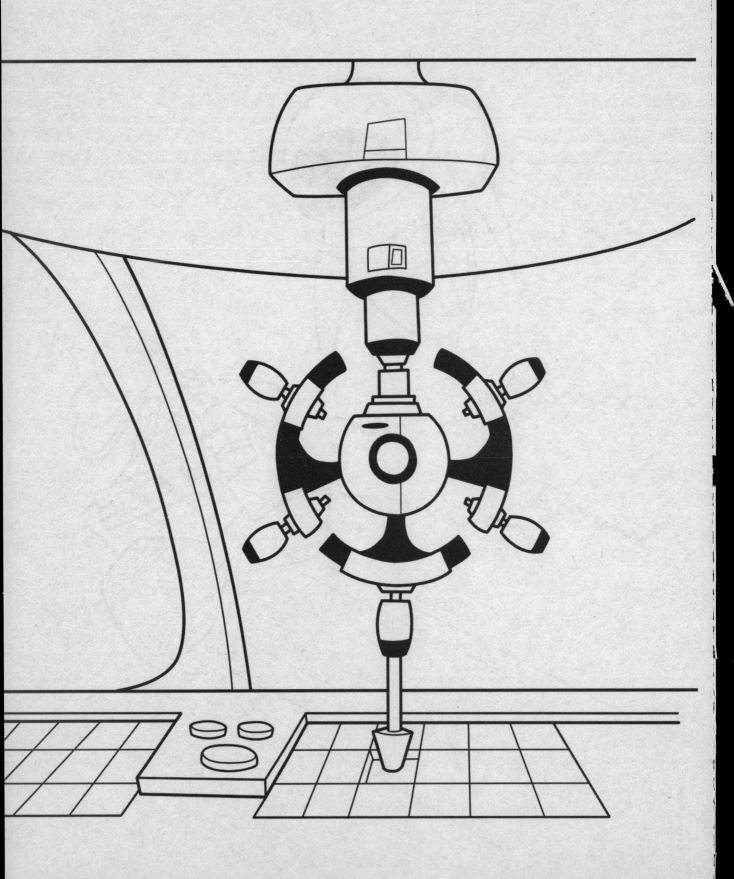

The Captain of the *Axiom* uses his computer
to learn about Earth.

Sparks fly between WALL•E and EVE.

M-O is on WALL•E's trail!

WALL•As are giant robots that cube trash—just like
WALL•E does!

M-O jams open the air-lock doors
and saves his friends.

All of WALL•E's friends are ready to help him!

This reject-bot and the security-bot face off!

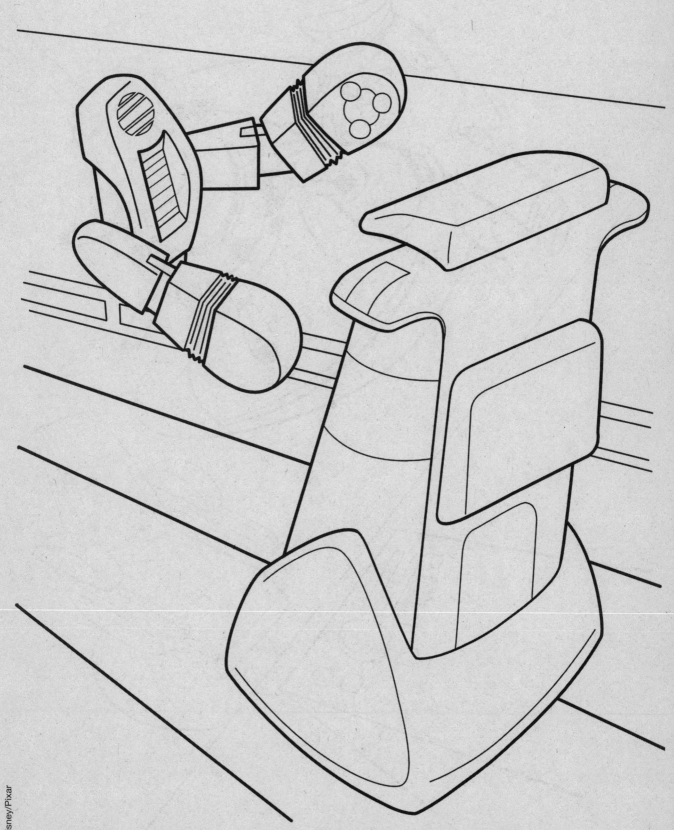

The Captain battles Auto for control of the ship.

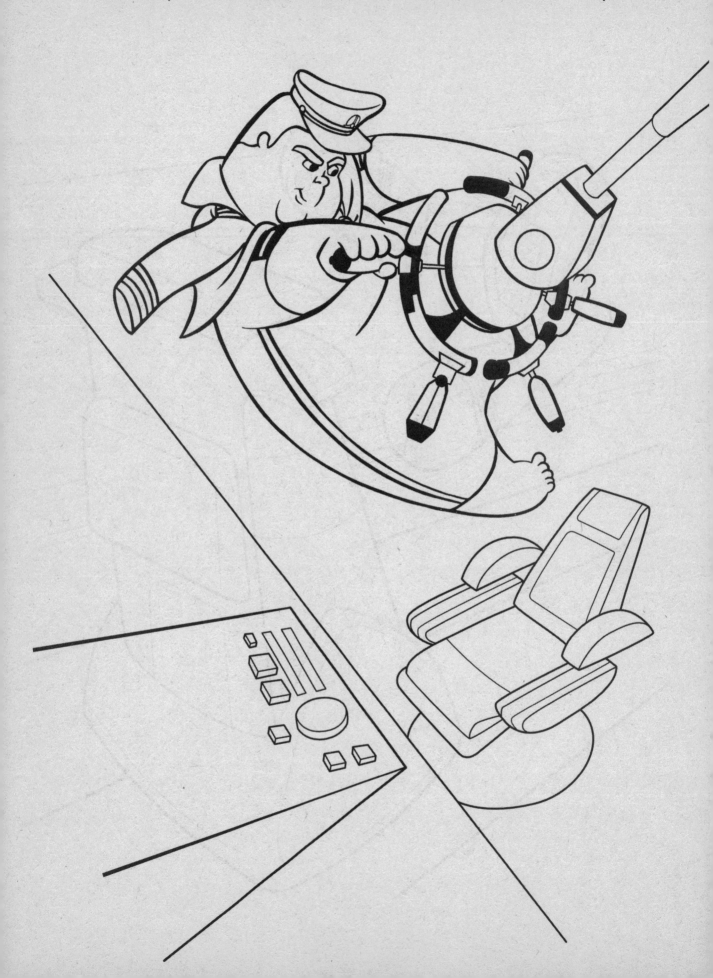

The Captain shuts Auto down for good!

WALL•E and EVE are happy when they return to Earth.

Russell is a proud Junior Wilderness Explorer.

Circle the two pictures of Russell that are exactly the same.

⑥   ①   ②

Russell

⑤   ③

④

ANSWER: 5 and 6.

When Russell tries to help an old man named Carl,
he gets carried away on Carl's floating house.

Russell has never been in a floating house before!

A big storm is coming, and Russell is ready!

Russell and Carl crash-land far from home.

Russell agrees to help Carl pull his house through
the jungle to get to Paradise Falls!

Russell meets a strange bird.

Russell names his new friend Kevin.

Carl doesn't like Kevin.

This is Dug. He is a dog with a special collar that allows him to speak with human words!

Russell likes to play with the buttons on Dug's collar.

Dug wants to take Kevin away. Kevin won't go!

Draw a line from each picture to its close-up.

① ② ③ ④

Ⓐ Ⓑ Ⓒ Ⓓ

ANSWER: 1-C; 2-A; 3-D; 4-B.

Alpha, **Beta**, and Gamma are looking for Kevin.

The dogs want to take Carl and Russell to their master.

The dogs belong to Charles Muntz, the famous explorer.

Poor Dug! The other dogs make him wear the Cone of Shame.

In each row, circle the picture that is different.

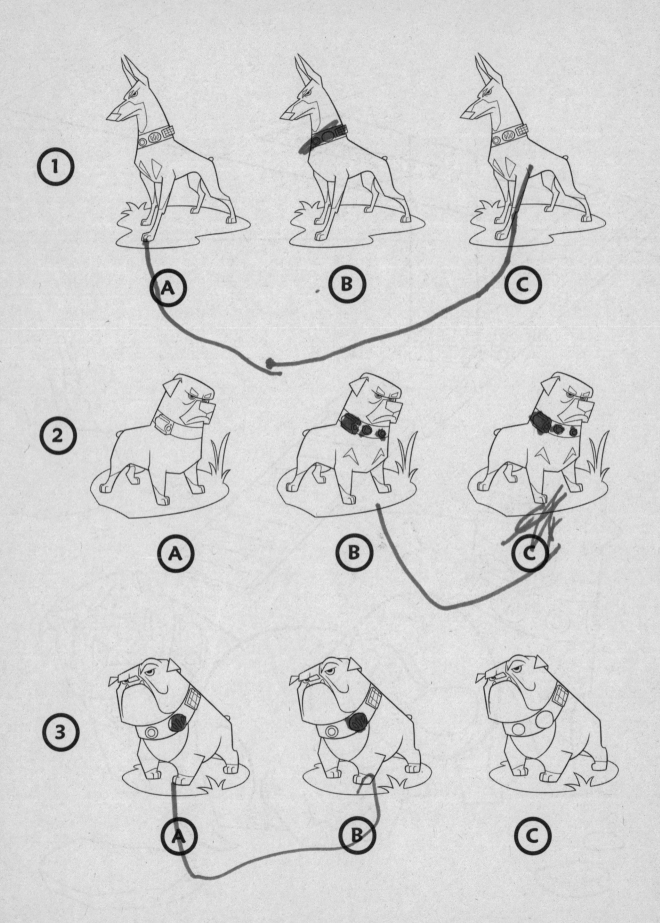

Aboard the blimp, Carl and Russell see all of Muntz's trophies.

Muntz wants to capture Kevin!

Kevin and Russell save Carl!

To help his **friends** escape, Dug pushes rocks into the dogs' path.